## *"What did you wish for?" Skye asked.*

Rose looked into his eyes, tried to memorize the tenderness she saw there. She remembered her birthday wish, its intensity and yearning. "Courage." She smiled. A tiny glowing spot of warmth in her chest took root and began to spread.

"Courage?" Skye regarded her quizzically. "Courage for what?"

"To do this, I think."

Like wisps of smoke, her fingers curled into his hair as she inched up and brought her lips to his.

Skye didn't move at all; he waited. His desire swelled to an aching need that encompassed every part of him—his mind, his body, his soul. And in every way the need felt urgent.

He had so many questions about her, but the first touch of her lips answered the most immediate of them.

*Yes,* she wanted exactly what he did.

Dear Reader,

What a month of wonderful reading Romance has for you! Our FABULOUS FATHERS title, *Most Wanted Dad*, continues Arlene James's miniseries THIS SIDE OF HEAVEN. Single dad and police officer Evans Kincaid can't quite handle his daughter's wild makeup and hairdos. Luckily—or not so luckily—the pretty lady next door is full of advice....

*Do You Take This Child?* is the last book of Marie Ferrarella's THE BABY OF THE MONTH CLUB miniseries—and our BUNDLES OF JOY title. Any-minute-mom-to-be Dr. Sheila Pollack expects to raise her baby all alone. But when the *long-absent* dad-to-be suddenly bursts into the delivery room, Sheila says "I do" between huffs and puffs!

In *Reilly's Bride* by Patricia Thayer, Jenny Murdock moves to Last Hope, Wyoming, to escape becoming a bride. But the town's crawling with eligible bachelors who want wives. So why isn't she happy when she falls for the one man who doesn't want to walk down the aisle?

Carla Cassidy continues THE BAKER BROOD miniseries with *Mom in the Making*. Single dad Russ Blackburn's little son chases away every woman who comes near his dad. It just figures the boy would like Bonnie Baker—a woman without a shred of mother material in her!

And don't miss the handsome drifter who becomes a woman's birthday present in Lauryn Chandler's *Her Very Own Husband*, or the two adorable kids who want their parents together in Robin Nicholas's *Wrangler's Wedding*.

Enjoy!

Melissa Senate,
Senior Editor

Please address questions and book requests to:
Silhouette Reader Service
U.S.: 3010 Walden Ave., P.O. Box 1325, Buffalo, NY 14269
Canadian: P.O. Box 609, Fort Erie, Ont. L2A 5X3

# HER VERY
# OWN HUSBAND

## Lauryn Chandler

*Silhouette*
R O M A N C E™
Published by Silhouette Books
America's Publisher of Contemporary Romance

For my mother, Laura Lea Warren.
Every day, you teach me a little more
about courage and love. Thank you for
always being my biggest fan. In case I
haven't told you lately, I'm yours.

SILHOUETTE BOOKS

ISBN 0-373-19148-0

HER VERY OWN HUSBAND

Copyright © 1996 by Wendy Warren

**Printed in U.S.A.**

**Books by Lauryn Chandler**

Silhouette Romance

*Mr. Wright* #936
*Romantics Anonymous* #981
*Oh, Baby!* #1033
*Her Very Own Husband* #1148

## *LAURYN CHANDLER*

Originally from California, Lauryn now lives in the beautiful Pacific Northwest, where she can look out her window and see deer walking down the street. She holds a B.A. in Drama and when not writing, enjoys spending time with her family and fiancé, going for long hikes with her dogs and finding new ways to cheat at Crazy Eights.

Lauryn is the recipient of the 1995 RWA RITA award for Best Traditional Romance.

# Five things a woman should do before her thirtieth birthday:

1. Kiss a cowboy.
2. Drink champagne at midnight.
3. Throw out, bury or burn all her flannel nightgowns.
4. Make sure her love life is the talk of the town—at least once.
5. Take a chance on someone...

# Chapter One

*Hurry, Mrs. Wyatt, please hurry!*

Rose curled her fingers tightly around the open drawer of her cash register as the old woman on the other side of the counter painstakingly counted out change.

"One dollar twenty-five cents, one dollar thirty-five cents..." Mrs. Wyatt's dentures clacked with each word. Her aged brow wrinkled as she fished through her purse. "I think I have a quarter in here somewhere...."

Gritting her teeth, Rose forced a smile to hide her impatience as the pile of coins swelled ever so slowly toward the five dollar mark. Tapping her foot on the floor, she shot a discreet glance at the clock above the lunch counter. Five minutes to closing.

*Hurry, hurry, hurry.* The single word drummed through her mind like a chant, but she clung resolutely to her smile.

In the ten years Rose had known her, Eula Wyatt had never carried anything larger than a fifty-cent piece in her purse, regardless of what she intended to purchase on a given day. Normally Mrs. Wyatt's penchant for small change didn't faze Rose. As sole proprietor of Wiedler Country Emporium and Café, she was used to her customers' idiosyncrasics. And usually she had plenty of time to cater to them. Life, after all, moved s-l-o-w-l-y in Wiedler, Arizona.

But tonight...

The second hand clicked to 5:56, and Rose's smile faltered.

Eula plunked a nickel onto the counter.

"Forty-seven." Down went another nickel. "Four dollars seventy-*five* cents..."

Rose realized she was holding her breath as Eula's forearm disappeared once more into the depths of her large handbag. Mrs. Wyatt always insisted on paying to the last penny—and pennies were usually what she came up with toward the end.

The round plastic clock that commanded Drink Pepsi across its white face lurched to 5:57.

Eula's gnarled fingers scraped along the vinyl bottom of her purse. "I thought I felt...wait a minute... Yes, here it is...." She withdrew her arm and there between her fingers was a silver coin, shining, Rose thought, like a beacon. "Let's see now, that makes..."

"Five dollars!" Rose blurted. "The quarter makes five dollars. That's perfect, Mrs. Wyatt." She began scooping coins into the register drawer with no concern for order, and Mrs. Wyatt frowned in disappointment.

"Aren't you going to count it?" A careful tally of the always-exact change was part of their daily ritual.

"I'm in a bit of a hurry tonight." Rose smiled apologetically.

"Are you coming to bingo, dear?"

"Not this evening, no." Without offering any information about what she *was* planning to do, Rose shut the register drawer, tore off the receipt and ushered Mrs. Wyatt to the door. A string of bells jingled against the glass. "I'll see you tomorrow, Mrs. Wyatt. Good luck at bingo."

Quickly Rose turned the key in the lock, flipped her We're Open sign to the side that read Sorry We Missed You, and turned to look at the clock.

6:01. She had exactly four minutes.

The emporium was divided into two sections, a lunch counter and kitchen on one side and a general goods store on the other. Rushing first to the store, Rose headed for the aisle where she stocked sugary snacks. Tapping a finger against her lips, she scanned the products, grabbed a package of Twinkies and hurried over to the lunch counter. Next to the glass jam pots she'd washed that morning and hadn't yet refilled, a package of candles sat waiting. She looked again at the clock—6:02.

"Plate. I need a plate." Mumbling to herself, she snatched up a small white dish, the candles and a slim butane lighter, then took her booty around to the customer side of the counter.

Tearing open the cellophane, Rose peeled one of the cream-filled sponge cakes off its cardboard square and set it carefully on the plate. She took three candles—one for each decade—out of the box and pressed them gently, almost reverently, into the Twinkie, lining them up in a neat row. Then, with her bottom lip caught between her teeth, she touched the lighter flame to the candles.

For just a moment as the short wicks caught fire, Rose felt as giddy as a child with a Fourth of July sparkler.

Smiling, she set the lighter on the counter and sighed.

*Oh, Rose, for a woman who's about to turn thirty in one minute, you're being awfully sentimental.*

Years ago, her grandmother had told her that if she made a wish at the exact time of her birth, the wish would come true.

Rose had believed it for years. Her grandmother would set out cake and ice cream, and together they would light the candles. At precisely 6:05 p.m., Rose would make her wish.

Oddly enough, even as a child she was careful to keep her wishes short and simple, careful not to ask for too much. Then sometime in her early teens, the ritual had ceased altogether. By that time there had been too much work and too much reality in their lives to bother with such fancies.

Until now. Now Rosalie Honeycutt needed another wish.

The death of her grandmother a year and a half ago had unmasked the loneliness Rose had held at bay for years. With the emporium to run and her grandmother to talk to, she had been able to pretend that her life was full...or full enough. But lately...

Lately the loneliness and the sameness of her days seemed almost suffocating. She had lost her sense of anticipation years ago, and the world, she had discovered, could be a dull place when you had nothing special to look forward to.

So for the past two weeks, she had looked forward to making a birthday wish.

"Barely thirty years old and you're getting dotty already, Rosie."

The clock clicked to 6:05.

Bending close to the candles, she closed her eyes. The warmth from the tiny flames touched her face.

"I wish," she whispered, clasping her hands and tucking them under her chin, "I wish...I wish..." She paused a moment.

What the heck, as long as she was acting silly, she might as well go for broke and make it a good one.

Putting her whole heart into it, Rose took a deep breath—and nearly shot off the stool when someone knocked on her glass door.

Swinging around, her heart thumping from surprise, she looked toward the sound.

It was dark outside. Most of the illumination came from a well-placed street lamp in the parking lot, but Rose could see clearly enough to know that the man peering through the glass—and right at her—was a stranger.

She didn't scare easily. In fact, she wasn't really scared now, she was...temporarily stunned.

The man outside was at least a head taller than the top of her Sorry We Missed You sign, which was hung at the five-and-a-half-foot mark.

He wore a faded denim jacket and a tan Stetson, both of which had seen better days. His jeans looked dark enough to be new, but they didn't save him from looking disreputable. Or, if not disreputable exactly, *well traveled*. His hair was too long; she could see the dark waves curling around his collar. His hat and the dim lighting worked together to create shadows that made it impossible to read the expression in his eyes, but she could see that he was tired. The kind of tired that gets in your bones. It was in his stance, in the slope of his otherwise broad shoulders, in the weariness around his mouth.

When she neither moved nor spoke, he raised his fist, tapped his knuckles once more against the glass, then pointed to his left. He cocked his head in question.

Rose had no idea what he was pointing at. Had his car stalled around the corner? Shaking her head to tell him she didn't know what he was asking, she stepped closer to the door.

"We're closed. Is there something you need?" She raised her voice to be heard through the thick glass.

The man nodded and though he didn't return her tentative smile, the stiff set of his mouth seemed to relax.

"I know you're closed. I'm sorry, but I saw your sign and I didn't want to wait until morning." His voice carried clearly, his register deep, the intonation slow and carefully measured.

*Even his voice sounds tired,* Rose thought, wondering which sign he was referring to. There was a Tan-Safe poster immediately to his left, but it was only February, so he shouldn't have a pressing need for suntan oil.

Maybe the two-for-one corn dog sign?

Wiedler was a tiny town whose local police blotter read like a day in "Mister Roger's Neighborhood." Growing up here had given Rose a sense of personal safety that might have been out of place in a larger town. As it was, her main concern was not that a strange man was at her door after closing, but that she was going to have to deny a poor, hungry traveler his corn dogs.

"I'm sorry." Raising her hands palms up, she shrugged apologetically. "The fryer's down for the night. There's a twenty-four-hour diner about a mile east—"

"No." He shook his head. "I'm not here for food. I saw your Help Wanted sign."

Rose's lips formed a soundless *oh.* When he tilted his head toward the sign, the light caught him full in the face, and she saw something she had missed before, when his features were hidden in shadows: he was beautiful. Not beautiful like a model or a movie star, but beautiful in a way that to Rose was purely romantic.

For years she had kept a poster hung near the cash register, a cigarette advertisement that showed a man leaning against a fence along a lonely stretch of road. He was wearing a Stetson and smoking a cigarette, and there was a backpack at his feet. Behind him, the sun was just beginning to rise.

A few years ago she had decided to stop selling cigarettes in her store, but she still had that poster, rolled up in a tube and tucked behind the winter rain gear in her hall closet. She couldn't bear to part with it because to her it didn't advertise cigarettes at all; it touted romance. The man on her poster was restless, a wanderer, and although Rose had never ventured far from Wiedler, she felt a kinship with him that began and ended in her very soul.

She saw the same restlessness on the face of the man on the other side of the glass.

"I'm sorry to be disturbing you, ma'am—"

*Ma-am?* She frowned. Lately more and more people had been addressing her as "ma'am." It made her want to run to the cosmetics aisle for face cream. Somehow at this moment she wanted very much to be considered a "miss."

"Your Help Wanted sign says to inquire within." A tiny, apologetic smile tugged at the corners of his mouth. "I didn't want anyone to beat me to it."

Rose nodded. Didn't want anyone to beat him to it, huh? She'd had that sign up for three months now, and he was her first nibble.

"Early bird catches the worm," she agreed, hoping he'd tilt his head to the light again.

"If you could tell me whether the job is still available, I'll come back first thing tomorrow morning to fill out an application."

Rose didn't answer him directly. He wouldn't want the job, anyway, when he heard what she was paying. And no doubt he was merely passing through on his way to greener pastures.

She stepped closer to the door. "You're not from around here."

Small as his smile was, it slipped from his face, and she realized that when he wasn't smiling, he tried not to show any expression at all. He was only partly successful: his features appeared immobile, but that didn't hide the fact that behind the blank slate he tried to create, thoughts obviously teemed.

She advanced until only the glass and a few inches of space on either side stood between them. "Where are you staying?"

"At the Good-Night Motel, across the street."

Rose nodded slowly. The old motel sat directly opposite the emporium. George Tilton, the owner, rented by the day, by the week and by the month. He never registered anyone who had fewer than three pieces of identification, and that increased her sense of security.

Reaching for the keys that dangled from a chain on her belt loop, she fitted a key in the lock. The bolt retracted with a loud click.

If he was surprised that she was willing to open the door to a stranger, he didn't show it. He backed up a step as she pushed the door out and kicked the doorstop into place.

With a brief nod of thanks, he entered the store. Rose flattened herself against the glass as he brushed past. They were face-to-face for no more than a second, but in that instant he looked directly into her eyes and smiled down at her.

Heat slithered up her neck and into her cheeks.

Most of the men in Wiedler looked like first cousins to Gomer Pyle, and as often as not they came into her store reeking of cattle. This man smelled of soap, like he'd just taken a shower. When he turned into the store, Rose saw that his hair was damp around the collar.

She swallowed hard and followed him in, leaving the door open. "I, uh, I have an application here . . . somewhere. . . ."

He turned from his casual perusal of the store, and she ducked down to rummage through a drawer below the cash register.

*Lord, he's handsome.* She'd never seen eyes like his. They looked like blue marbles.

Having decided years ago that she was plain as dry toast in the looks department, Rose found now that physical attractiveness fascinated her. When she saw it in such abundance in someone else, she felt something akin to awe.

"Here they are." Straightening with a triumphant smile Rose handed her prospective employee an application. "Do you need a pen?"

He nodded. "Thanks. Mind if I take this to the counter to fill out?"

"Help yourself."

Rose stood where she was, watching his broad back. He walked halfway to the counter and stopped. Turning around, he looked at her curiously. "Ma'am, if I'm keeping you from something, I can fill this out at the motel and bring it back tomorrow."

She shook her head. "You're not keeping me from anything."

When he frowned and looked toward the counter, she followed the path of his gaze. "Oh, my candles!"

Rose rushed to the counter, but all that was left of her birthday celebration were three melted stubs and a Twinkie covered in wax.

Sadly, she reached out, pressing a fingertip into the soft wax puddling atop the little cake.

The man beside her shifted and she looked up at him. He stood with one hand splayed across his hip, his frown settled on her makeshift birthday cake. When he brought his gaze to hers, his dark eyes were filled with an expression that she recognized immediately.

Pity.

It made her stomach clench. The last time a man had looked at her like that—with pity in his eyes—she'd felt so sorry for herself she'd married him.

Rose could tolerate feeling sorry for herself from time to time, but she couldn't stand anyone feeling sorry for her. She threw a curt nod at the paper in his hands.

"Mister, if you want to be considered for the job, you'd better get started on that application. I'm making my final decision tonight." She turned to gather the plate and candles.

"Yes, ma'am."

"And don't call me ma'am!" Spinning around, she glared at him. She was only thirty, for heaven's sake! "My name is Rose."

Carrying her plate around the counter, she scraped her Twinkie into a bus tray.

"You can sit at the counter."

He didn't answer, but took himself to the stool she indicated, a few counter spaces away.

As he clicked the pen and scanned the application, Rose glanced at him covertly. He kept his head bent over the page, so she couldn't see his expression.

*Not that he'd have one, anyway,* she thought sourly.

Tossing the package of candles next to the hot cocoa machine, she scowled at her own petulance. *You're getting prickly in your old age, Rosalie. The man saw you celebrating your birthday on your own. He wouldn't be human if he didn't have some opinion about that.*

Normally she didn't dwell much on what strangers thought of her. She'd learned at a young age that being average had its perks. Nobody expected great things from her, so there hadn't been much to live up to. She'd never felt like she had anything to prove.

Again she glanced at her prospective employee. He didn't lift his eyes from the page.

Another perk to being a plain woman was that you didn't feel disappointed when a man failed to notice you. Male eyes did not follow her as she worked behind the counter.

Not like the poor Renlow twins. Their breasts were so large, they had to pay property tax for residing in two states. When those girls came into the Emporium at lunchtime, there was so much drooling at the counter, Rose had to bus it with a string mop.

Now she, on the other hand, could go about her business freely, wearing jeans and no makeup if she chose and no one ever seemed to notice.

Take this very moment, for example. If she were a betting gal, she'd wager that she could stand directly opposite Mr. Stoneface and he'd never even see she was there.

Grabbing a damp bar towel, Rose wiped along the already clean counter, edging her way to where Stone Boy sat hunched over his application. She lifted the salt and pepper shakers and wiped beneath them. Then she picked up the napkin holder and wiped beneath that. She found a spot of dried ketchup on the yellow Formica and worked at it with her nail.

Nothing. Not a flicker of awareness that she was standing in front of him.

Just as she'd expected, Mr. Expressive didn't so much as bat an eye in her direction. Which proved her point, of course: Rosalie Honeycutt could stand on her head and sing "Let Me Entertain You" and still not attract undue attention from the male of the species.

What a relief.

Plastering a determined smile on her face, she slapped the bar towel into the bus bin and looked again to the man at her counter. Yes, indeedy... what a blessed relief.

Skye kept his head bowed over the employment application. Damn! The woman—Rose—was making him jumpy as a cat. This was the first application he'd filled out in ten years, and it was hard enough without her hovering in front of him.

She'd been nice enough when he'd first walked in, but something had pissed her off royally since then. Maybe she was upset about spending her birthday alone. Hell, he'd spent plenty of them solo.

When he sensed she was looking the other way, he glanced up surreptitiously.

Pretty, he thought, then wondered *why* she was celebrating alone. Her nut brown hair was pulled into a ponytail and Skye decided in a flash that he'd like to see it hanging free.

She had the face of a woman, well-defined and rich with expression. He liked that, too, although at the moment her expression was a little bit . . . dour. Her top lip was caught between her teeth and her brow pursed in a scowl. She looked, he decided, like she was afraid he was going to rip off her stainless steel napkin dispenser the minute her back was turned.

He lowered his head and tried to focus on the page again.

*Afraid he was going to rip her off.*

That was, of course, the crux of his difficulties with this application. He'd forgotten the sixty-four-thousand-dollar question that appeared on most applications for employment: Have you ever been convicted of a felony?

Perspiration gathered on Skye's forehead. He clicked the pen several times in rapid succession until he realized what he was doing and lowered his nervous hand. Rubbing his knuckles on the rough denim covering his thigh, he pondered his options in answering the question.

*Yes* or *no* were the obvious choices. *What's it to you?* came in a distant third, and *None of your damned business* would feel good, but ought to be ruled out.

How badly, he wondered, did he want this job? Badly enough to drag the past into the present?

When he'd rolled into town around three o'clock today, finding a job had been the furthest thing from his mind. He'd checked into the motel across the street, gone to his room, opened the curtains and sat in a chair for two hours, staring out the window at the comings and goings of Wiedler Country Emporium and Café.

He'd recognized most of the people who went in and out of the store—not *who* they were, but *what* they were. He'd grown up in a town quite like this.

Her customers were mostly old folk and ranchers, people who'd known each other for years and showed it in the way they interacted—chatting amiably outside the store, waving to each other in a casual I'll-see-you-again-later way.

As the sun had set and the foot traffic on the street outside the motel had grown quiet, Skye had decided to go for a walk. He'd crossed the street for a closer look at the Country Emporium and when he saw the Help Wanted sign, he felt a sense of anticipation that bordered on urgency.

Now, even though the store was empty save for himself and Rose, he realized he'd guessed right, about the sense of community and belonging people experienced here. The feeling lingered, as did the faint aromas of coffee and hamburger.

Skye felt his stomach start to growl and sucked in his muscles in an effort to quiet the rumbling.

For whatever crazy reason, he wanted any job she had to offer. The next few weeks were going to be hard, the toughest of his life, and he wanted to have this place to come to each day. He wanted to know he belonged somewhere.

His fingers tightened around the pen. The feeling of needing something so badly left a bitter, metallic taste in his mouth.

With the muscles tensed in his jaw, he bent over the page... and put a hard, angry check in the No box—no, he'd never been convicted of a felony. Even unspoken, the lie tasted like gall.

He completed the rest of the application swiftly, put the pen on the counter, stood and thrust the paper at the woman. The moment she reached for it, he let his hand drop, stuffing both his fists into the pockets of his denim jacket.

The woman's gaze dropped immediately to the application, and she scanned the page. Skye felt like he had hot coals in his shoes.

Turning on his heel, he managed to grumble a semi-polite "Good night, ma'am" on his way to the door.

"It's *Rose!*"

The growled reminder stopped him in his tracks.

Slowly, he turned around.

With her eyes blazing and her chin jutting out, the woman behind the counter looked ready to do battle. Her lips tightened, and he saw that she was gripping his application so tightly, she was crumpling it.

"Are you or are you not interested in this job, mister?" Her words were short and sharp. Skye looked at her curiously.

"That's why I came in, ma—"

Her eyes narrowed dangerously.

"Rose," he corrected.

With her gaze still narrowed, she tilted her head to one side. "Well, for someone who says he wants a job, you sure have ants in your pants."

Skye felt a reluctant smile lurk around his lips.

"The hours are 8:00 a.m. to 3:00 p.m. I don't need you after three because things get slow in the afternoon. Any problem with that?"

A tiny, dawning ray of hope stirred in his chest.

"No."

"Can you start tomorrow?"

Slowly he nodded.

"Good." Seeming to realize for the first time that she'd crushed his application, she smoothed it against the apron tied around her waist. "Don't bother to have breakfast tomorrow. You can eat when you get here."

Skye had felt grateful, truly grateful, just twice in his life: once when his friend Sully offered him a job and a new start on his dude ranch . . . and right now.

His chest, throat and face filled with a puzzling warmth, a physical sensation generated solely by emotion. He wasn't used to it.

When he spoke, his voice was quiet and rough. "Thank you."

She nodded brusquely. The interview appeared to be over. Skye turned toward the door again, but he knew he couldn't leave without saying one more thing. Whether she realized it or not, the woman had just given him a jolt of confidence and a sense of belonging and purpose he was going to need badly in the coming weeks.

Allowing a smile to form and widen until he was actually showing some teeth, Skye infused as much sincerity as he could into a voice too used to speaking perfunctorily. He looked right in her eyes, large and brown, and nodded slowly.

"Happy birthday, Rose."

# Chapter Two

The rich aroma of fresh coffee, the hiss and sizzle of frying bacon, and the woodsy, sweet scent of warm maple syrup filled the Wiedler Country Emporium and Café as it did every morning at breakfast time. By 7:00 a.m. on the most ordinary day of the week, the customers around Rose's counter had mouths filled with food and faces graced by satisfied smiles.

But today was no ordinary day.

Millard Walsh, who had been coming to the emporium since Rose was in pigtails, took a large mouthful of coffee and nearly spewed the sludgy brew over the counter. He looked at the pancakes Rose had set before him and decided they bore a striking resemblance to the flat tire in the bed of his pickup. To top it off, the grits he'd ordered—and had thoroughly enjoyed every morning for the past twenty years—were hard as cement and about as tasty. He turned to his left to see if his old buddy Ray was faring any better.

One glance at Ray's plate had Millard slapping his gnarled fingers against the counter.

"Good God Almighty!" His crackly voice carried clearly down the row of customers and to Rose, who was pouring more pancake batter onto the griddle. "What in crying out loud's wrong with you this morning, girl? I could hammer a horseshoe against these grits, and Ray's eggs 'n' onions is so raw, I'm going to be chewin' on his breath all day." Millard shook his head in disgust. "I don't know what you've got your mind on today, Rose, but it sure ain't cookin'!"

Rose dropped the ladle she was holding into the bowl of pancake batter. Millard was staring at her like his suspenders were too tight, and Ray looked as sad and confused as a bulldog puppy who'd lost his bone. The other faces around the counter were equally somber.

Lowering her gaze to their plates, Rose realized with chagrin that she'd burned the toast and barely cooked the eggs. And the grits did look a little ... solid.

Setting her bowl of batter aside with a grimace, she hurried to collect their breakfast plates and begin again.

Millard pinned her with a penetrating stare. "You got a bee in your bonnet today, Rosie?"

Avoiding his gaze, she flashed a nervous grin and shrugged. "My timing must be off, Mill. I'll fix it."

Beneath bushy, Albert Einstein brows, the old man's eyes narrowed suspiciously.

Rose turned away. Mill knew her better than anyone else in town. He'd been her grandmother's best friend and her own greatest source of support when Lilah died. But what could she tell him now? *"I'm on pins and needles because I'm sure the man I just hired won't show up—and if he doesn't, I'm afraid I might burst into tears."* That would surely make her sound like she'd

spent too much time under the hair dryer. Especially since
the man she'd hired was a total stranger who, as far as she
could tell, had no pertinent job experience.

Even after reading his application, Rose knew next to
nothing about Skye Hanks. He'd answered every question as briefly as possible. All she'd gleaned was his age—
thirty-three, the fact that his past jobs had included
"traveling" and "working with horses," and that a man
named Sullivan Martin was his only reference, personal
or professional. In response to the question "Why are
you leaving your present position?" Mr. Hanks had
written a terse "Want a change."

As job applications went, this one wasn't sterling. Still,
though the information had been sparse, it was not altogether unenlightening. It perfectly fit Rose's image of
the romantic wayfarer she believed she'd hired, and it
whetted her appetite to learn more about him.

Last night when he'd smiled—so softly and so sin-
cerely—and quietly wished her a happy birthday, she'd
felt... heck, it was embarrassing, but... well, *melty* inside. Something weathered and tired within her had
turned nervous and young in an instant.

She liked the feeling.

For the first time in years, life seemed fresh and new
again, crackling with possibilities.

Feeling a blush coming on, Rose turned to the pancakes that were bubbling on her griddle.

Oh, she was some piece of work, all right—a thirty-
year-old woman who went loopy because a simple
"Happy birthday" had rolled off a man's tongue.

Except that the words hadn't seemed simple; and they
hadn't exactly *rolled*. She had sensed the vulnerability
and the gratitude behind the rough monotone, and she
guessed that words did not come easily to Skye Hanks.

Slipping a spatula under the pancake with the most bubbles, she lifted it from the griddle to flip it over.

"Hello."

The deep baritone came from directly behind her. Rose jerked around, and the pancake seemed to jump off the spatula of its own volition. It landed on the hard linoleum floor, wet-batter-side down.

"Aw, for cryin' out loud." Millard shook his head. "First pancake of the day that had any potential." He turned to the stranger who slid onto the stool to his right. "Fella, if I was you, I'd grab a pack of Scooter Pies and hold out till lunch."

Skye Hanks glanced from Millard to Rose. His brow lifted. "That right?"

Rose felt the blush filling her freckled cheeks. She wanted to smack Millard right on top of his fuzzy gray head.

"Morning," she mumbled, sending Skye an abbreviated smile. Nervously, she looked for something with which to wipe up the pancake. "Breakfast'll be a few minutes, but I'll get you a cup of coffee."

Millard winced at the mention of this morning's brew. He nudged Skye with his elbow and warned in a loud whisper, "You'll be takin' your life in your hands today, son."

Rose shot her old friend a quelling glare and bent to scoop up the fallen flapjack.

As she mopped the floor with a towel, she couldn't help but acknowledge the trembling excitement and relief she felt at Skye Hanks's arrival. He was going to work here!

He had dressed for his first day in a blue cotton work shirt with pockets on the breast. His collar was open. Even the quick glance Rose had given him revealed that he had hair on his chest that was as dark as the hair on his head. Without his Stetson, his attractiveness was fully revealed.

His hair was thick and black; it curled rather than waved. In the daylight, his eyes were a startling blue at which the night had only hinted. But it was the shape and strength of his square jaw and chin that would have given him the look of a *GQ* model in cowboy garb, if not for the world-weary, edgy aura she'd noticed again this morning.

Straightening without making eye contact, Rose turned to the coffee machine to embark once more on the morning meal. She was conscious of the voices behind her and fumbled with the coffee filters when Millard asked Skye if he'd been in town long. Keeping her back to the men, she measured the coffee carefully and waited for Skye's answer.

"I got in yesterday." His voice was brusque, not inviting of further conversation, but Millard persevered.

"Just passing through?"

"Not exactly. Excuse me, sir."

The urge to turn around to see where Hanks was going almost overwhelmed Rose, but she forced herself to concentrate on the coffee.

*Not exactly just passing through.*

And not exactly staying?

Rose frowned. As his employer, she had a right to ask what his plans were.

When a finger tapped her shoulder, she jerked in surprise.

Mr. Hanks had come around the counter and was looking down at her with the first glint of real humor she had seen in his eyes.

"Looks like I'd better earn my breakfast today. If you make the coffee, I'll get started on the breakfast orders."

Rose's brows lifted in surprise, then just as quickly lowered in concern. She'd hired him to help around the store, as a stockboy and cashier. She'd never dreamed— especially after reading his application—that he would help out at the counter.

"Do you know anything about fry cooking?" Doubt laced her voice.

He nodded toward the griddle behind them. "I know those pancakes are burning."

"Oh, no!" Dropping the coffee scoop, Rose rushed to save her flapjacks. Not a one survived. They were raw on the top and burned on the bottom. Millard grumbled behind her. "Shinola! If this ain't the darnedest morning around here."

Aflame with embarrassment, Rose began scraping away at the griddle with a spatula. A large, tanned hand covered hers.

Skye said nothing. He simply took the spatula and finished the job of cleaning the griddle with ease.

"If you show me the tickets, I'll get started on the pancakes and the eggs."

Rose blinked at him without moving. Her hand, Lord help her, was tingling where he'd touched it. She stood there, wishing he would smile, and he stood waiting for her to give him the breakfast tickets, until Ray spoke up in his thin, high voice.

"You gone and hired somebody, Rose?" When she didn't answer right away, his voice got higher and thinner. "Have ya? You workin' here, young fella?"

There was a near imperceptible lift to Skye Hanks's dark brow—a question, Rose thought, and she gathered the tickets of the meals she hadn't yet made or was forced to remake, handing them over with a shaky smile.

"If you do the pancakes and eggs, I'll get the bacon, toast and potatoes."

He accepted the tickets with a slow nod of agreement. "Sounds good till I know my way around."

A bucket of eggs, the bowl of pancake batter and a plate stacked with three unwrapped one-pound cubes of the real butter Rose used for frying were all within his reach. Rose longed to stand there, watching him work, but she wisely moved on to her own tasks, sensing that he preferred to work without being watched.

As she got started on the coffee again, she caught Millard's eye. He looked at her curiously, but said nothing, for once allowing the other regulars to comment in his stead.

"So, you finally got some help around here. Well, ain't that nice..."

"Guess the prices'll be goin' up now you've got a hand to pay, huh, Rosie?"

"You gonna be a tough boss to work for, Rosalie?"

There was much teasing and a good deal of unspoken curiosity about the newcomer as Rose and her employee worked the counter.

It was delivery day for the two supermarkets in town and a number of familiar truckers stopped in, adding to the ranks around Rose's counter. For the next two hours, there was no time for chatter.

Skye never lost a beat. He worked smoothly, rarely appearing awkward in his actions, except when he was searching for something that wasn't readily visible.

He turned out pancakes that were uniformly golden and round; he cooked eggs any way the customer required, and they were always perfect. When given a compliment, Skye nodded politely, but in two hours, he didn't utter more than a dozen words.

When the heat of the breakfast rush ended around nine-thirty, Rose poured him a cup of coffee and told him to sit down.

"You never did get breakfast."

He hesitated. "I've got two more orders to fill."

"I'll do it."

Rose raised the mug, and the aroma of strong, fresh coffee drifted to Skye on a swirl of hot steam. She could see that he was tempted, but a glance at the clock told him he'd only been working two and a half hours.

He shook his head.

"Thanks for the coffee." Reaching over her hand to place his fingers around the rim, he took the mug from her. "I'll have it while I work."

Rose frowned. "You'll sit down and have breakfast."

For the first time this morning, she sounded like a boss.

"I promised you a meal," she insisted, "and we're going to have to clean up in a little while to get ready for lunch. There won't be another break until two o'clock." She crossed her arms over her chest. "I don't want you reporting me to the labor board."

Watching her over the rim of the cup, Skye took a sip. As he swallowed, Rose could almost feel him savoring the warmth and flavor.

At last he nodded. "I'll take ten minutes, if that's okay."

"You'll take twenty minutes," she countered. "Sit down and I'll bring you something to eat. It could be a long afternoon. We're running a special on all-you-can-eat spaghetti."

He hesitated a moment longer, then a near-imperceptible smile tugged one reluctant corner of his lips, and he moved around to the customer side of the counter.

Rose watched him slide onto the same stool he'd taken earlier that morning, which meant that once again he was seated beside Millard.

Generally, Millard and Ray left the counter by nine to sit out front and play checkers or to make their rounds of the other shopkeepers in town. Today no amount of coaxing by Ray had been able to budge Millard, and finally Ray had left on his own.

Now Mill sat nursing his coffee, his sharp gray eyes brimming with curiosity. It wouldn't be long, Rose knew, before the old man's friendly prying began.

She hurried to fill the remaining breakfast orders, including Skye's. If there was going to be prying going on, she wanted to be there to reap the benefits.

As she heaped home fries onto a plate laden with sausage links and three scrambled eggs, she pondered the change in her attitude from yesterday to today. Yesterday morning if someone had asked her, "Rosie, how would you like to bake biscuits and fry potatoes for the rest of your days?" she would have burst into tears at the very prospect. Today she saw her biscuits as a creation, her potatoes as a work of art. Even the smiles on her patrons' faces seemed brighter to her and if someone had told *her* to take a break, she would have asked, "What for?" The past couple of hours had flown by like mere minutes.

Skye's eyes widened when she set his plate on the counter, and Rose knew a moment's deep satisfaction when he closed his eyes briefly and inhaled the aroma of fried potatoes and onions and piping hot biscuits. She hovered nearby as he took his first bite.

Next to Skye, Millard pursed his lined lips, took a sip of coffee and studied Skye. He smiled as the younger man bit into a fluffy, hot biscuit dripping with butter and honey.

"Good, ain't it?"

Apparently not one to speak with his mouth full, Skye turned his head and nodded politely.

Millard smiled, displaying a row of straight teeth that had seen their fair share of tobacco and coffee. "Rose's biscuits is the best there is."

This time Skye made direct eye contact with Rose. He nodded again.

Millard warmed the palms of his hands around his coffee cup. "So, you hired on . . . when? Last night?"

Skye swallowed, and Rose found herself fascinated by the play of muscles in his neck. "Yes, sir."

Rose busied herself with tucking plastic wrap around the butter, but she listened to every word.

Millard blew on his coffee, took a noisy sip and set the cup down with a solid *clunk*. "Good thing you showed up when you did," he told the younger man approvingly. "Rose was so busy watchin' the door, she about poisoned us before you got here." He cocked an eyebrow at his longtime friend. "Were you afraid he wouldn't show up?"

Coloring furiously, Rose glared at Mill, who smiled in return. Skye glanced up from the sausage he was working on, but his expression remained impassive.

Mill leaned forward on his elbows. "I saw Eula Wyatt at bingo last night." He cocked his grizzled head at Rose. "She said you were in some all-fired hurry to get out of here. Where were you goin'?"

Rose glanced from Millard to Skye and back again. The memory of her lonely, aborted birthday commemoration did nothing to increase her comfort around her handsome employee. "Nowhere," she mumbled, wiping toast crumbs off the cutting board. "I just wanted to close on time for a change."

She checked the level of Mill's coffee cup, grabbed a towel and mopped up the milky ring the ceramic creamer left on the counter. "You regulars think you can hang around half the night. Someone's got to break you of the habit."

Millard harrumphed. "If that's a hint, I ain't takin' it." He winked at Skye like they were old chums. "So what were you in a hurry about? Somethin' good on TV?"

Rose tried not to cringe. His inference that she didn't have anyplace—or anyone—interesting to rush home to was embarrassing to say the least. It was also the truth, which made it all the more irritating.

Summoning a noncommittal smile to her lips, she collected Mill's coffee cup and started toward a bus bin.

"Hey, I'm still drinkin' that!" He stopped her, affronted. "Boy, somethin' sure has you walkin' around cross-eyed this morning. If this is going to happen every Friday, I think I'll eat at the diner—" Struck by a thought, Millard stopped himself mid-sentence. His exaggerated facial reaction made him look like a cartoon character—eyes bugged wide, lips open, bushy brows raised so high his eyelids weren't sagging for the first time in years.

"Holy cow." He whispered the words the first time and then repeated them so loudly, every head at the counter, including Skye's, turned in his direction. "Holy cow!"

He slapped his palm against his weathered forehead.

"Well, if I ain't a horse's patoot . . . what day is this?"

He wagged his head, then dropped his hand and looked dolefully at Rose. "Yesterday was March the second, wasn't it? I'm sorry, darlin'. I must have cow patties between my ears. How could I have forgotten your birthday?"

"It's no big deal." Rose kept her voice low and dismissing, casting Millard a glance that asked him to please drop the subject.

"'Course it's a big deal!" Mill's booming exclamation ensured that every customer at the counter was listening to the exchange. "A gal's birthday is always a big deal. Ain't that so?"

He nudged Skye's arm.

Reluctantly, as if she were compelled to look against her will, Rose glanced at Skye.

His left arm rested on the counter alongside his plate. His right hand curved around his coffee cup. He'd rolled up his shirtsleeves in order to work. Rose noticed first that his forearms were broad and muscular, covered with a masculine fur as dark as the hair on his head. Next, she noticed that the same hair peeked from beneath the open V of his collar.

Her gaze rested there a moment, then traveled up past his square chin and the firm line of lips, which, as usual, showed little expression.

Her gaze moved higher, until she was looking directly into his eyes.

She'd seen a lot of blue eyes in her day: pale and faded—the blue eyes of the aged; sharp, twinkling, knowing—cowboy blue; but never had she seen eyes like Skye Hanks's. His eyes were dark—the blue of a moon-lit midnight sky. They were by turns mysterious, world worn, ironic—but always intense. Always watchful.

He was watching her now. The steadiness of his gaze made her think for a moment that he was no longer aware of the chatter going on around them.

Abruptly, forcefully, Rose felt like she was sucked into the eye of a storm. There were no sounds outside her—and no noises in her head, either. For the present, the inner turmoil, the chattering disquiet was suspended. All that existed was the sensation that the two of them were alone in the room, a strange, dreamlike feeling—at once calming and electrifying.

When Millard's voice intruded on the peace, Rose was startled and disappointed.

"We could have a party tonight." His suggestion was met with a chorus of agreement that shook Rose from her reverie. "We'll have it at the senior center," Mill decreed. "Who wants to bring the cake?"

"I will," Claire McCoy, seated three stools down from Skye, offered without hesitation. "And I'll bring some of those John Denver tapes my granddaughter gave me."

"Good," Mill agreed. "And we'll need paper plates and plastic forks. Who can bring those?"

"I can." Flo Arnold, one stool away from Claire, piped up. "And I have some hats left over from New Year's. One is a beautiful cardboard tiara with silver glitter. I made it myself," she beamed. "Rose can wear that one since it's her birthday."

Skye's brow lifted ever so slightly.

*I want to leave.* Rose couldn't help it; she cringed inside. *I want to get out of here before someone suggests playing Pin the Tail on the Donkey.*

These people were her friends and, Lord knew, they had the best of intentions. But cake and punch and cardboard tiaras? She was thirty, not eight—and not eighty-eight! Women her age drank champagne out of crystal flutes; the most she could hope for was purple Kool-Aid from a Dixie cup.

Emotion constricted in her throat.

Breaking eye contact with Skye before she humiliated herself further, Rose turned her back to the counter.

She shouldn't have hired him.

What could a drifter do but remind her that she was as grounded as he was free; moored to this town, to this counter, to this surpriseless existence; bound more by fear of the unknown than love of the familiar.

"We need drinks." Oblivious to Rose's dilemma, Millard kept organizing. "Punch. The cherry kind."

Rose closed her eyes.

"We need paper cups, too. Eight ouncers, not them little bitty ones...."

She closed her eyes tighter, squeezed them to keep the tears from slipping out.

"So who's bringing the drinks?" Millard asked again, his enthusiasm growing with each new detail.

And, in a voice that was quiet and sure, Skye Hanks answered, "I am."

# *Chapter Three*

There were two automated teller machines in Wiedler, one on Fifth Street, sandwiched oddly between Betty Jane's Hair Artistes and a pizza parlor called Frank DeRoma's, and a second machine in front of the bank on Main.

It was the latter location Skye chose for his first fiscal transaction in Arizona, a twenty-dollar withdrawal to buy punch for Rose Honeycutt's birthday.

He'd put in a good day's work at the emporium, not as long or as hard as his days on the ranch, or the bone-rattling hours he'd spent riding enraged bulls, but a day that left him tired and satisfied in a way he couldn't quite name.

Reaching into the back pocket of his jeans, he pulled out a brown leather wallet so old and creased it was worn white in spots. The damn billfold was near to crumbling. He should have replaced it years ago, but it had been a gift from his friend Sullivan. Sully had handed it to him along with his first paycheck for working at the Lazy G.

Extracting his bank card, Skye inserted it into the machine, pressed the appropriate buttons and took his cash. He tucked the bill neatly away. No matter how much or how little he had, money was something he never took for granted. The people who had it made the rules. Sully— who had plenty of it—had understood that.

Rubbing his thumb over the cracked cowhide, Skye knew he would keep the wallet till it was worn as thin as the bills it held. His lips curved in a wry smile. A wallet, a paycheck and a bedroom without bars—life's simple pleasures.

Returning the wallet carefully to his pocket, he started up Main Street toward Van Allen's Market.

He couldn't remember the last time he'd gone to a birthday party, but by hell he'd be there tonight.

Rose Honeycutt. He grinned. Damn, but she was a piece of work. Particular as hell about where the butter went and whether the grill was cleaned just right, but she'd give the whole damn store away to the first person who came along and asked real nice, he could see that. She was bossy and prim and . . . kind.

Skye slowed his step and breathed the clean desert air. Kindness.

Now there was a quality he hadn't come up against in a long, long time. It left him feeling slightly off-balance.

Nine years ago when he walked out of Garret Federal Penitentiary, Sullivan Martin had treated him fairly and decently. On the rodeo circuit he had known people who were eager to give him pretty much whatever he wanted, once he'd made a name for himself and a fistful of money. But that wasn't kindness.

Kindness was letting a nine-year-old kid named Mac stuff napkin holders in return for a meatloaf supper he took home to his family. Kindness was burning the toast on one side only for Mrs. Rollins and charging Mr. Lewis a dime for coffee because the old man thought it was still 1952.

A sudden gust of wind stirred the palm trees lining Main Street. Skye hunched his shoulders against the high-desert chill.

The encroaching twilight was deep blue-gray and cloudless. He gazed at the infinite blue and remembered a pair of eyes exactly that color. He blinked as he remembered, too, another time in another place, on his twelfth birthday when gentleness had been the rule in his life, not the exception....

*"Take your finger out of that frosting young man, or your birthday party will be canceled due to circumstances beyond your control."*

*Skye peeped up at his mother and grinned. Slowly, ever so slowly, he dragged his finger out of the milk-chocolate frosting she'd spread over his birthday cake.*

*Raising a chocolate-covered finger to his lips, Skye studied his mother's expression, grinning more broadly still when he saw the dimple appear in her right cheek.*

*"Don't do it," she advised, but laughter belied the warning in her words as his tongue snaked slowly out to taste the frosting. It was a game now and they were both enjoying it.*

*Finger and tongue inched closer.*

*"I'm warning you, mister...."*

*Skye seldom disobeyed the major rules in his mother's home, and she always took minor infractions—like frosting tasting—in stride. She loved his teasing almost as much as he loved to tease her.*

*"Mmmm."*

*He licked his finger clean in an instant, and the next moment she was chasing him around their small apartment, from kitchen to living room, around the brand-new used sofa their upstairs neighbor had given them and into the tiny dining area his mother had decorated with red balloons and crepe paper streamers.*

*When he let her catch him, she tickled his ribs and growled into his neck and kissed his cheeks until he swore never to swipe frosting again.*

He never did.

As far as Skye could recall, he'd never even considered sticking his finger in another birthday cake.

He'd never gotten the chance. Four months after his twelfth birthday, his mother was gone—"passed on," they told him, as if a "passing" was less awful than a death.

Skye, too, had passed on then, to a life so different it had been hard sometimes to believe he was still living on the same planet.

A strong sense of self-preservation had led him to bury the memories of the gentleness he had known. To remember love and kindness in a life so suddenly devoid of either would have driven him crazy.

Loving hadn't come easily since that time, either. He'd tried—and failed so miserably, he'd nearly ruined his own life and a couple of others in the bargain.

The heels of his cowboy boots clicked in a steady rhythm against the sidewalk. He paced slowly and thought.

He'd been free for nine years now, free to travel down any street he chose, free to use an instant cash machine.

But freedom, he had discovered, was a relative thing.
And there were other kinds of prisons, with bars you
could not see.

He didn't want to get involved in the lives of these
townspeople. He had enough to do while he was here
without complicating his life any further. But he'd felt
comfort today... and peace. In some strange unspoken
way, Rosalie Honeycutt let him taste both again, if only
for now. That deserved more than a few cans of punch.


"Keep your eyes closed!"

"She can't see nothin', can she, Mill?"

"Don't you peek till we tell you now, Rosie."

Peek, shmeek. With all the pushing and tugging she
was suffering at the hands of Millard, Ray and Mrs.
Wyatt, Rose figured she'd be lucky if she didn't break her
neck.

"I can't see anything through this scarf," she assured
them, twitching her nose as the material they'd tied
around her eyes started to slip.

It was beyond her why they wanted to blindfold her
just to enter a senior center multipurpose room she'd
been in dozens of times, but it seemed important to them,
so she played along.

Now Eula was giggling and Ray was fairly skipping
with anticipation, and Rose found their excitement con-
tagious. They must have pulled out all the stops: streamers from Easter, hats from the Fourth of July, the
balloons they had left over from Willa and Bob Jen-
kins's thirtieth anniversary party. More than likely, the
room would look like a party-supply-store, half-off sale.

And they were doing it all for her. Rose felt guiltier
than ever for greeting their initial proposal with something less than undiluted enthusiasm. So her life didn't

consist of champagne sipped at midnight and cruises in spring; at least she had friends with keys to the multi-purpose room.

Rose smiled beneath her blindfold. Ray had one of her hands, Eula had the other, and Mill brought up the rear, nudging her every couple of steps like she was a mule with its hooves in the mud.

"Halt!" Millard directed as they reached the double doors leading into the center. Rose heard Mill hustle around her and felt the soft swish of cool air as he opened the door. Music poured out the door in jubilant greeting.

"Okay, look now!" Knobby-knuckled fingers reached for the blindfold. Rose blew her mussed bangs from her eyes and blinked to focus her vision.

She gasped at the sight before her.

Lights! Hundreds of starry, twinkling lights winked at her from wire cords strung in gently dipping rows from the center of the room.

Tables bearing food, refreshments and gifts were set up along the perimeter. On the stage that the Wiedler Community Players had built at the far end of the room, Mac Ridley and the Blowhards, a group of local businessmen and erstwhile musicians provided music to dance by.

And by gum, as Mill would say, that's exactly what everyone was doing. Clara Welchel was fox-trotting with Vern DeWitt, the Schultz family was dancing together in a circle, and the Holt sisters were moving in short, choppy steps and arguing about who was supposed to lead.

Slack-jawed with awe, Rose glanced around the broad room. Dear and familiar faces creased with smiles when they spotted the guest of honor. She couldn't think of a person she knew well who wasn't present and accounted for. The knowledge that they had done this for her, created this starry eve in a senior center multipurpose room, filled her heart with gratitude and her eyes with happy tears.

With a hand on her chest, above the rapid, glad beat of her heart, Rose turned to Ray, Mill and Eula. "Oh, thank you," she breathed. "It's just beautiful. I don't know how you did it with only a day to plan."

"Less than a day," Eula piped up, proud as a hen on a three-pound egg.

"And so many people are here!" Rose turned back toward the room. "However did you get word to them all?"

Ray offered one of his gummier grins and held a forefinger up for her inspection. "My dialing finger may never be the same."

"Mine, either." Eula elbowed him in the ribs. "Leave Rosalie go now. Everyone wants to say hi."

Ray offered Eula his arm and together they moved into the room. Several people broke from the crowd and were heading Rosie's way. She looked quickly at Mill, wanting to give him special thanks. He took no credit, but she knew he was the organizational force behind the party.

"No wonder you never came back for lunch."

Millard smiled, his eyes twinkling like the Christmas lights strung across the room. "We-ell . . ." Hooking his thumbs in his belt loops and rocking back on his heels, he let the word roll out in a teasing drawl. "A man learns how to ignore his stomach over the years, when there's work to be done."

He grinned broadly. Rosalie grinned back. They both knew he hadn't missed a meal in fifty years.

"Seems to me a gal who works as hard as you do deserves a party." He paused, sobering slightly. "Lilah would've wanted you to have one."

In that moment, Rose felt like her grandmother was at the party with them.

Mill wasn't comfortable with physical displays of emotion, so Rose settled for a whispered "Thank you," as three people descended to pull her into her birthday party.

An hour and a half later, she had accepted good wishes, two cups of punch and three invitations to dance—the last from Sparky Owens. Sparky was the skinniest man in Wiedler, but he could two-step like nobody's business.

When they finished their dance, Sparky delivered Rose to the food table and to Mill, who was busy sampling one of everything—several times.

He smiled as Sparky trotted off for another dance. "That boy must have been born with jumpin' beans where his toes oughta be."

Rose fanned her hot cheeks with her hand. Keeping up with Sparky was hard work, all right. She nodded at the stuffed celery Mill was popping into his mouth. "Looks like you worked up a good appetite, yourself. I saw you dancing with Rietta Nix."

Millard's grin was positively wolfish. He bent his knees and dipped a couple of times. "These old bones still have some give." He reached for a Vienna sausage roll. "Lord, I love a potluck. I won't have to eat again till next Tuesday." He raised his brows at Rose. "Not that I won't still drop by the counter."

Rose nodded wryly. "I'm not worried."

Finishing the sausage, Mill licked mustard from his fingers, glanced down at his full stomach and sighed with regret. Turning away from the buffet, he stood next to Rose and surveyed the guests. "Yup, good turnout. 'Course it's your meatloaf special that got everybody here on such short notice. I told 'em you were switchin' to liver 'n' onions unless you got a party."

Rose laughed. Mill crossed his still-burly arms over his chest, pretending not to notice that Anita Whitehall was giving him the eye from the dance floor.

"So, you think your new hand'll relieve your workload some?" Mill queried casually.

The question caught her off guard. She had just spotted the employee in question. More than an hour into the party, and she still hadn't spoken to Skye. Not even to thank him for bringing the punch.

She'd been aware of his presence all evening, of course. He'd been there on the fringe of the party, standing alone or talking with one of the single women present.

Apparently the single women of Wiedler had made it their mission to see that Skye felt welcome. And they certainly knew how to go about it, Rose acknowledged. Some of them were barely out of high school, but they hovered over him with the dedication of guardian angels, the vigilance of...

*Pitbulls*. Rose felt a scowl she was helpless to unfurl settle across her brow as Annie Renlow, Amy's twin sister, took her turn vying for Skye's attention. She was leaning into him, her hands on his arm, her blond head tilted back as she gazed at him. Skye wasn't smiling, but he didn't look too upset, either. And why should he? Annie Renlow's chest was snuggled against his upper arm. His bicep was probably in heaven.

"I said, you think life'll be easier at the store now?" Millard repeated.

"Much." Her scowl dropped lower. Annie had pressed herself so closely to Skye's side that their hips were touching.

Ripping her gaze from the couple, Rose stared grimly into her punch. It was as red as Annie Renlow's lips.

Red lips. Touchy hips. Other women had them, but not her. There were aspects of womanhood that seemed utterly beyond her grasp and always had seemed so. The very thought of flirting filled her stomach with a thousand butterflies. Trying to talk to a man she was attracted to made her feel like she'd eaten too much sugar.

Lifting the punch to her lips to give herself something to do, Rose bit down onto the rim of the plastic cup.

It was so damn frustrating! If only she could take life—and herself—less seriously, forget her fears and her rules and have the fun she saw other people having. And, Rose thought, her teeth still clamped on the cup, Annie certainly looked like she was having fun.

"I ever tell you how Gummy Brenner got his nickname?" Millard cut into the depressing line of her thoughts.

"No. How?"

"Chewin' plastic cups. Wore his teeth down to nubs. Has to gum all his food."

Rose lowered the cup from her lips. "That so?"

"Yup." Mill let her chew on that for a while, then said, "Somethin' about that new hand of yours bothers me."

If Rose didn't know better, she would have sworn her ears swiveled in Mill's direction. "Oh?"

"Yup." His eyes narrowed. "Seems familiar somehow. Anything about him seem familiar to you?"

*Only that he looks and smells and walks like every fantasy I've ever had.* "No. I never saw him before Thursday."

"I didn't say I'd seen him before. Said he seemed familiar." Mill shrugged, but he continued to watch Skye.

So did Rose.

Disengaging his arm from Annie's, Skye took a step away, said something Rose wished she could hear and headed for the doors. He walked with a firm, directed stride, like there was something outside he wanted. Or like there was going to be.

Annie stood where she was for a moment, then wove her way through the crowded room and followed him out the door.

It took every ounce of self-discipline Rose possessed not to run after them to see where they were going.

She tried not to glare at the door, but feared she was failing.

How tawdry.

How cheap! Imagine arranging a rendezvous with someone you just met at a party.

*And it's my party! If anyone has a rendezvous, it ought to be me!*

Putting her cup on the table before her tense fingers crushed it, Rose grimaced.

Fat chance that she would ever sneak out of a party to meet a man. She had too many rules, too many standards for that. Too much fear. . . .

Millard nudged her arm. "Look at that." He nodded toward the dance floor. "Sparky is doin' the Charleston. Ain't his legs just made for that?"

Rose nodded. Sparky looked like a pipe cleaner twisted in several directions at once.

Mill made a clucking sound with his tongue. "Funny a good dancer like Sparky never got married."

Rose shrugged. Good dancing. Wouldn't it be wonderful if that was all it took to make a marriage work—a few lessons at an Arthur Murray studio and you'd have a partner for life.

At least Sparky was kicking up his heels these days. Back in high school Sparky Owens had been her study partner in chemistry lab.

He had also been her only date in high school. They were a good match, both hopeless in chemistry and equally awkward in the social realm. They went to the junior prom together. Rose's grandmother was more excited than either of the kids. She bought a new roll of film for the Polaroid camera, and Rose hadn't had the heart to tell her that Sparky had been planning to go miniature golfing with his friends that night and only agreed to attend the prom when Rose promised him a week's worth of her grandmother's plate-size cinnamon rolls if he would escort her. It had taken her weeks to work up the nerve to ask him.

He didn't kiss her good-night at the end of the evening, but Rose didn't take it personally. In eleventh grade the only person more shy than she was Sparky.

"Well, I'll be..." Mill murmured and Rose once again followed his gaze.

"What?" She frowned. "What are you looking—" But then she saw. Annie Renlow had returned, shoving through the doors of the multipurpose room.

"She looks madder than a hornet with his stinger in a sling." Mill chuckled.

Rose agreed. Annie's rosebud lips were compressed into a tight, flat line. Her bleached brows were drawn together and her eyes were shooting sparks like Fourth of July sparklers as she wove her way toward her sister.

Except for her expression, nothing else seemed amiss. Not a strand of her cotton-candy hair was out of place, her scarlet lipstick was neither feathered nor smeared and her skinny red dress was right where it had been before—barely hanging on to her outrageous curves.

"I wonder what happened?" Rose mused aloud.

"It ain't gonna be Annie Renlow, that's what happened." Mill grinned. "Ray just lost a buck."

"What?" Rose turned to him. "What are you talking about?"

Mill's grin turned mischievous. "We was wonderin' this afternoon who Hanks was gonna take up with. Got a pool started. Everyone put in four bits."

"A pool?" Her eyes widened in surprise. She felt vaguely appalled... and wildly curious. "That was fast work, wasn't it? You only just saw him today. It took you longer to get a pool going for the Super Bowl."

Long, deep grooves creased Mill's cheeks. "This is more interesting."

Rose fingered one of the small plastic buttons on her blouse. "Who all did you bet on?"

Mill rubbed the gray stubble that no amount of shaving could keep at bay. "Let's see, so far there's three bucks down on Annie, five on Amy Renlow, two on Jemma Lee, and Eula's got a dollar on Flo Gibbons—all in nickels." He leaned toward Rose and spoke out of the side of his mouth. "Wishful thinking if you ask me. Flo's only a year younger than Eula."

Mill continued, ticking off names of the women who had so far garnered single-dollar bets.

"Mmm." Rose frowned. She made a studious examination of the nail she'd broken earlier that day opening a canning jar of spiced peaches. "Who'd you bet on, Mill?"

The grooves alongside his mouth deepened.

"Laura Michaels. She's a pretty little thing, and I hear she's got a wild streak in her."

"Oh." *Chin up. Would you really want someone to bet on you like you were a racehorse?* "Sounds like you've got quite a pool going."

"Yup."

Rose looked away. Mac Ridley cued the Blowhards to begin their rendition of the Beatles' "When I Saw Her Standin' There." For the first time this evening, Rose lost track of whether Skye was in or out of the crowded room. For the first time this evening, she didn't care.

"It's getting kind of hot in here." Raising her voice to be heard above the music, she motioned to the doors. "I think I'll step outside for a minute."

Mill peered at her. "You okay? Your face is kinda splotched."

"I'm fine. I just need a little air."

Tossing a limp smile Millard's way, Rose headed for the doors. She thought someone called to her, but she didn't bother to stop or even look up until she was outside the senior center, leaning against the cold, solid wall, letting the darkness and the shadows soothe her.

She had known for years, of course, what they all thought about her. Everyone in Wiedler knew that romance stuck to Rosalie Honeycutt about as well as water on an oil slick.

Eight years ago Dwyer Simms had married her for ten weeks, and when he blew out of her life and out of town he took with him the last bit of courage she possessed.

Over the past eight years, she had taken the plain, artless girl she had been when Dwyer left and, with conscious deliberation, had become even plainer.

Dressing plain, talking plain—Rose had built a wall of unconcern that locked out the pain of hoping, always hoping. With all the thoroughness she could muster, she had buried the woman she might have become, sealed the lid on her passions... and went numb.

For a while it had seemed to work. She was Rose the fry cook, Rose the business owner, Rose the friend. Rose the woman had all but disappeared, and with her, the woman's feelings.

But now something was backfiring. Because living numb was starting to hurt.

Closing her eyes, she leaned her head against the wall. The thick elastic band holding her hair in place pressed into the back of her neck, reminding her that her hair was still in a ponytail, the same style she'd worn earlier today—and the day before that and the day before that. Straight, unadorned. A nothing-special style for a nothing-special life.

Reaching up, she grasped the coated rubberband between her fingers and pulled it from her hair in one swift, disgusted move.

She didn't stop to think. Hooking the elastic over her left thumb, she used her right forefinger to pull the band back, and—

*Zing!* she let it fly, and it went zooming into the darkness. There was a satisfying *snap* on the release and an equally satisfying snap when it made contact with... something.

"Ow! Son-of-a—"

The colorful exclamation came from deep in the shadows. Rose leaned forward, eyes wide and wondering until, moving out of the darkness and into a slice of light,

Skye Hanks appeared. He held one hand cupped over his right eye.

Walking toward her until there was only a short, neat space between them, he stared at her in pained disbelief, one dark brow thundering over his uninjured eye.

"Nice hit . . . *ma'am.*"

## Chapter Four

"Oh, dear heavens!" Rose's hands went to her mouth. "Are you all right? I didn't see you. What were you doing skulking around out there?"

Her tone went from apologetic to accusing in less time than it had taken to snap the rubber band. The vulnerable area beneath his eye stung like a son-of-a-bitch, but Skye found himself smiling. The irony of it all struck him as fairly humorous.

He'd been standing in the dark, wiping the unwelcome imprint of Annie Renlow's iridescent lips off his neck and contemplating taking up smoking again, when Rose emerged from the party. He hadn't been able to see her well—she had chosen to stand in the shadows, as had he—but he was pretty certain he'd heard her hiccup, a woman's kind of hiccup that sounded like she was trying not to cry out loud.

The ability to comfort was not one of his natural gifts. He couldn't remember ever exercising it before. He hadn't even been certain how he was going to go about it, but he'd walked toward her, drawn by an unfamiliar need.

And then—*smack!* Struck down in his first attempt to do a good deed.

He lowered his head as a chuckle, an honest-to-goodness chuckle tumbled in his chest.

"What's the matter?" Rose grew worried when his shoulders started to shake.

Grasping his wrist, she pulled his hand away from his face. The first thing she saw was his smile.

"You're laughing." Irritation replaced the fear in her eyes. "I thought I really hurt you!"

Skye kept his right eye squinted for effect and raised his left brow. "Well, it didn't feel good."

Immediately, concern returned. "I'm very sorry. Did it hit you right in the eye?"

She was truly worried, and it showed. Taking pity on her, Skye opened his eye and shook his head. "No. It's okay."

He stood quietly then, just watching her. Her hand was still clasped around his wrist, but he knew she was unaware of it. Her fingers were long and cool.

Annie Renlow had pressed a lot more than fingers against him, but it hadn't felt this good.

He'd watched Rose during the party and had found himself contrasting her with other women then, too. There was something different about her, something that made him think of the daguerreotype he'd seen once of Sully's great grandma in her youth, like Rose didn't fit the time in which she lived.

Always, she carried herself like a lady. When she laughed with her friends, when she picked something up from the buffet, when she danced with the tall, skinny guy... she was a lady all the way through.

She even smelled like a lady, he realized now. She smelled, he thought, like her name, though the scent was so faint he wondered if he might be imagining it.

She was still studying him with genuine concern. He liked that, too.

*Rose... Rosalie...* Regret filled his chest. *You're a lady, and I'm no gentleman, and the timing's all wrong.*

He thought of the fury she'd put into snapping the rubber band and smiled.

"You must have had some powerful need to change your hairdo," he commented softly, raising his hand to her neck. Her hair fell like a chocolate waterfall here. Pretty. Simple. Slowly, sensing he might scare her if he moved too quickly, he ran a finger gently along the curtain of hair.

Rose held her breath.

She'd only just become aware that she was holding Skye's hand... or was he holding hers? Either way, she felt powerless to do anything about it. She could barely think with him standing so close. And the way he looked at her...

Goodness gracious, what was happening? He was looking at her as if... as if...

*Stop!* She screamed the warning at herself before another daydream had the chance to get a toehold. *He is a cowboy and a drifter, and Annie Renlow got his motor running. He'd probably look at Eula Wyatt the same way he's looking at you, if she were out here right now.*

She focused on her track record where men were concerned and vowed not to make a jackass of herself.

"I like your hair."

"You do?" She swallowed hard. *He likes... he likes...*

Skye nodded.

Rose stared.

"You wear it down much?"

"No. Sometimes."

He nodded more to himself than to her, his expression thoughtful. The gentle smile faded. "Sorry I didn't get you a gift."

"A gift?"

"For your birthday."

"Oh." Her ears were buzzing. "That's all right."

Skye smiled again, wryly this time. "It's always good to keep the boss happy."

*Uh-huh.* Rose felt her heart thumping as her fuzzy brain scrambled for something to say. If she were one of the Renlows, she'd be flirting right now.

She wasn't a Renlow. Even before Dwyer, flirting had made her feel clumsy and foolish.

"Uh—" she began.

"I'd better let you get back to the party." Less slowly than he'd raised it, Skye let his hand fall away.

"See you tomorrow morning." He tipped his head to her respectfully, as he might have tipped his Stetson. "Happy birthday, Boss."

He turned and sauntered through the moonlit parking lot.

Rose watched him—broad back, narrow hips, long legs.

She shivered. She felt cold and hot at once. Every pore on her body tingled, like she was standing in a thunderstorm with her face to the breaking clouds.

He said he was sorry for not giving her a present. But he had. With a look and a touch and words softer than any she had heard before, he had brought her back to the world of feelings and longing. Rosalie Honeycutt wanted something again.

As quickly as she'd made the vow not to be a jackass, she forgot it. After all, where there was hope, there might also be fulfillment.

Rose stared glumly at the reflection in her mirror.

"I look like Laura Ashley on Valium."

Her pink blouse and pleated skirt were the color of bubble gum drying on cement. The blouse sported white buttons shaped like flowers and a sweet lace collar that resembled the doilies she used to line the doughnut tray.

This was the first time in years she'd "dressed" for work and her outfit looked like she'd picked it up at a convent yard sale.

One week had passed since the evening of her party. One week, and Skye hadn't mentioned her hair—or any other part of her—since then.

He was hard working, considerate, quiet and kind. How she had come to admire and enjoy his kindness! The particular brand of courtesy and respect he exhibited when dealing with people told her more about him than if he'd attached an autobiography to his résumé.

That first night after the party, she'd lain awake, wondering if she'd only imagined the admiration and gentleness in his steady blue gaze when he'd said, "I like your hair." Simple words, but they had power. They reached past every defense she'd built up over the years and curled around her heart.

Before Skye Hanks arrived, her future had looked like a low-desert landscape—no peaks, no valleys. Now she had more than mere hope; she had something to hope for. She wanted to see that look in his eyes again and to feel those feelings. Today. Now.

"Did you really like my hair?" Rose whispered into the mirror and imagined Skye nodding, his sober eyes and enigmatic half smile enveloping her.

Rose kept her grandmother's silver brush and comb set on top of her oak dresser. She reached for the brush, watching herself in the mirror as she ran the bristles through her brown locks. Her grandmother, Lilah, had been blessed with striking auburn waves which had remained richly colored well into her sixties. Rose's own shade seemed drab by comparison. In truth, she seldom paid any attention at all to her own hair.

Lilah had spent long minutes in the evening dreamily pulling the silver-backed brush through the tresses she had always refused to cut.

*"Your grandfather gave me these right after we were married,"* she would say, cradling the comb and brush in her strong hands. *"He brushed my hair every night of our married life."* As always when she reminisced about Rose's grandfather, Lilah's expression would grow misty and faraway. *"That's what I wish for you, Rosalie, dear. A man who will brush your hair... every night...."*

What a simple wish, Rose thought, running her fingers over the intricate silver back.

Lilah, she knew, had felt great pain as she watched her only grandchild retreat farther and farther into her shell after the debacle of her brief marriage.

As she had seen her grandmother do so many times, Rose hugged the brush to her. "You were the lucky one, Grandma."

Lucky, she thought, and brave. It took courage to throw oneself into life—day after day, year after year.

*If only,* Rose thought, *I was prettier.* Lilah had been a lovely young woman; old photographs of her attested to that. Did prettiness make life easier? Did it make a person braver?

What would it take to attract a man like Skye? Because that's what she wanted to do. She wanted more of last Friday night... and then some. She wanted to share secret looks, to have him catch her glance in the middle of the breakfast rush and give a slow, lazy smile, just for her.

He would raise a dark brow and nod toward the food aisle. Silent communication. *Meet me later... behind the chips and salsa, baby.*

Grabbing a white headband, Rose slipped it on, tucking the tips behind her ears. Not exactly a glamour look, but it would keep her hair out of her face while she cooked.

Studying herself in the mirror, she tried to see what Skye had found appealing that night. Turning her head from side to side, she searched for a certain angle, a way she might have tilted her head—

There! If she dropped her head to the right and tilted her chin left, her hair fell in a nice shiny curtain.

The cuckoo clock in the living room chirped six times, and Rose realized she should have been downstairs setting up for breakfast fifteen minutes ago. Living directly above one's place of business had its drawbacks, but the commute to work was not one of them.

Tentatively, she directed what she hoped was a flirtatious smile toward the mirror.

Skye had noticed her once when she hadn't even been trying to be attractive. No telling what could happen today if she put her mind to it.

She winked at the mirror, and her smile expanded to a grin.

* * *

"What's the matter with you? You sleep bad last night?" Millard peered at Rosie as she refilled the ketchup bottles.

"No." She wiped the mouth of a bottle with a damp towel.

"You got a crick in your neck?"

"No."

"Then why's your head all bent over?"

Rose pursed her lips and clapped a top on the ketchup. "It's not bent over," she grumbled, putting the freshened bottles on the counter.

Okay, so maybe she *was* starting to get a crick in her neck. It was eleven o'clock, and Skye had barely offered her a civil word yet, much less a lingering look. The more distant and elusive he seemed, the more angles she tried with her head.

As for secret smiles and intimate communications—zippo. His most intimate communication so far had been a grunted question about the cinnamon rolls.

In the face of his disinterest, Rose's optimism was seeping away like water from a cracked bucket. Verbal flirtation was out of the question—she could barely summon a syllable—so she'd been resorting to angles for the past two hours.

Chin down, head tilted left; chin up, head right. Nothing seemed to make an impact on Mr. Hanks.

*And no wonder,* Rose thought tartly, adjusting her white headband and rotating her neck to work out the kinks, *I look like Alice in Wonderland trying to hide a goiter.*

In another hour they would be smack in the middle of the lunch rush, and there wouldn't be any time to talk.

She looked toward the front of the store, where Skye was stocking candy. His jaw was locked and he was frowning—his standard expression this morning.

"Well, I'm shovin' off." Mill drained the last of his coffee. "See you tomorrow, sugar." He pushed off the stool.

Contrite because she knew she'd been distracted all morning, she politely followed Millard to the door and waved him out, but even then her attention was on Skye, who was crouched before a small box.

Rose watched him break the seal with his hands, rather than using the X-Acto knife to which she usually resorted. He had on a pale green cotton shirt today, with the sleeves rolled halfway up his strong forearms. His muscles bunched as he popped the box flaps. Rose didn't even try not to stare.

Skye stood to refill the candy rack.

Telling herself there was no reason that an attractive man should make her nervous, she walked toward him. "You've been working hard today."

Looking up, he nodded politely.

She twisted the towel she carried tightly around her fingers and cleared her throat. "I really appreciate your working so hard. I wouldn't have gotten to those candy racks until next week. You make things a lot easier around here."

"Good." Skye shoved a box of chocolate-covered caramels onto the rack. He smiled.

Rose unwound the towel from her fingers, reached for a box of pecan logs and set it on the rack next to the caramels. "You don't take enough breaks, though."

"I had breakfast."

"Yes, but you ate in ten minutes. That's not good for the digestion." Fidgety, she wagged the towel from side

to side. "We'll be a bit slower this afternoon than we were
yesterday."

"Why's that?" he asked, stocking marshmallow treats
and peanut butter bars.

"Oh, Frank DeRoma runs a pizza special at his place
every Friday. Buy a large, get a medium free. Or buy one
medium deluxe—that's three toppings—and you get a
pitcher of whatever you want to drink. It's a good deal.
I can't beat it."

Absently making room on the rack, she took the peanut butter bars and moved them to their rightful place
next to the caramels. "Frank's pizzas are the best in Arizona."

He turned, resting an elbow on the top of the rack and
giving her his full attention for the first time today. "That
so?"

"Yes." She laughed, little half-voiced puffs that were
breathy and nervous because she'd suddenly realized
what she was working up to. "That's what it says on
Frank's menu, anyway."

Skye watched the dimple appear in Rosie's cheek and
cursed himself for walking into this store. Half the time
she looked at him like he was someone special—someone worthy of a woman's attention. No one ever looked
at him like that, anymore. He grabbed another box and
shoved it onto the shelf.

The simplest damn things felt personal when he was in
her presence. And he wasn't a personal kind of guy. Like
the day she'd insisted on his using antiseptic when he cut
himself with a paring knife. Hell, he could have bled to
death a dozen times over in the past years and no one
would have fussed. But she cared about everything, and
the problem was he liked it.

"By the way, how's your eye?"

Skye gritted his teeth and steeled himself against the pure gratitude he felt every time he heard concern in her voice.

"Fine," he responded shortly. She'd asked about his eye every day for the past week.

"Too bad the accident didn't happen in the store," Rose mused. "Then you could have asked for workman's comp. Not that I have workman's comp," she remembered, pursing her wide lips. "My grandmother and I were the only people who worked here for years, so we never needed it. Do you think that'll be a problem?"

"No," Skye said flatly, but he found that he disliked the idea of Rose and some frail old lady hefting large boxes around the store. Sexist or not, he decided that from now on, he—and only he—would handle the heavy lifting.

Rose noted the return of his scowl with a sickening discomfort and came close to losing her nerve.

Hopelessly naive regarding the art of flirtation, she decided she had the ideal discreet invitation, a way of asking Skye out that could easily be construed as casual. Clearing her throat, she took a leap of faith.

"Well," she ventured, mouth and throat dry as dust, "since I can't offer you workman's comp, how about one of Frank's famous pizzas?"

The last words came out in a pinched, nervous croak. Rose heard it. Skye heard it. She swallowed convulsively. So much for casual. She felt like a statue in an earthquake—stiff and trembling at once—and knew for a fact that as long as she lived she would never again ask a man out. Without doubt, ten years had just been cut off her life. Even if he said yes, was it really worth it? The way her heart was racing, they'd have to deliver the pizza to intensive care. And if he said no—

"Wait here."

*Wait here.* Rose blinked. Was that a yes or a no?

He strode away.

Rose waited, surprised and immobile for a brief moment, then started after him, craning her neck to see around his broad back.

Two young men who had eaten a late breakfast at the counter were huddled together in one of the beverage aisles. Skye headed straight for them, stopping just a few feet away.

"Put it back."

He issued the order casually, but there was steel beneath the words. Steel and warning.

The boys, most likely in their late teens, turned around. Rose stood slightly behind Skye. She had no idea what he suspected the boys of taking, but she could see by their expressions that he'd caught them red-handed.

"Put what back?" The taller one, with shoulders almost as broad as Skye's and his hands stuffed into the pockets of a weathered letterman's jacket, glared in belligerent surprise.

Rose couldn't see Skye's face, but she felt his deliberate pause, as if he was deciding whether to be reasonable.

He nodded to the smaller teen, who wore an army jacket. "Take the can of beer out of your pocket and put it back on the shelf."

The boy exchanged a glance with his friend, then bared his teeth in a smile pregnant with disrespect. "Beer?" He laughed. "Man, what's your trip? We don't have any beer."

Rose dragged her upper lip between her teeth and watched the three men face each other down. Skye was larger than the shoplifters, but not by much. Anger vibrated among the three of them, and she didn't want it to escalate, not over a stupid can of beer.

Stepping forward so they would shift their focus to her, she offered what she hoped was a placating smile. "If you boys will come to the cash register and show me your IDs, I'll sell you the beer. Otherwise, you're welcome to help yourselves to a soda, on the house."

With a note of icy warning and the hardest look she had seen in his eyes yet, Skye contradicted her. "They'll put the beer back and *buy* a soda if they want one." He leveled his metallic gaze on the teens. "Now."

The confidence of the smaller kid, the one Skye apparently suspected of possessing the beer, wavered a bit. The taller and more belligerent of the two held on to his sneer.

"What's the matter with you, man, you got wax in your ears? We already told you, we don't have any beer. And if you dee-tain us and you're wrong, you could get sued." He narrowed his eyes lazily. "Now is a little can of beer—which we don't even have—worth that kind of trouble?"

Standing slightly behind him, his friend seemed to take courage from the disdainful challenge. He grinned again and tossed a cocky nod in Rose's direction. "She's the thief, man. She shouldn't charge for her food, she oughta buy us a beer for makin' us eat that—"

Skye's arms shot out, his fists closing around the collars of both their shirts. The rage quivering in his muscles seemed barely contained.

"Apologize," he ground out. "Then put the beer back on the shelf and get out. If I ever see you in here again, you'll wish I'd let the sheriff handle it. You understand?"

It was his fury, finally, that seemed to overwhelm them. Skye gave them each a sharp jerk when their responses seemed slow in coming.

"Start with the apology," he directed. *"Now."*

"Sorry," the shorter one mumbled, his eyes on Skye.

"Say it to the lady," Skye corrected, nodding toward Rose.

"Sorry," he mumbled again.

"Sorry," the other boy echoed, but his hostile gaze stayed on the man holding his shirt.

Slowly Skye relaxed his grip and released them. The two stood uncertainly, as if they weren't sure what was expected next.

"The beer," Skye coached.

The boy in the army jacket reached into his pocket. He withdrew the can and, moving gingerly, replaced it on the shelf. Skye jerked his head toward the door.

Clearly eager now to be done with the attempted theft and to get out of the store in one uninjured piece, the smaller boy ducked his head and skirted between Rose and Skye. His friend followed, but more slowly and without averting his head.

Rose watched them go, unable to relax until the door, with its rope of bells, jingled shut behind them.

She expelled a tense sigh and put hand to her chest. "Now you really deserve that pizza," she said on a shaky laugh and with no motive this time except to express her gratitude. "My gosh, I was getting scared. For a second there, I didn't think they were going to back down. I—"

She stopped abruptly, realizing that she was talking to herself.

Skye stood motionless, his hands balled into tight fists by his sides. He moved not an inch, not a breath, and yet his body seemed to vibrate with some potent emotion.

From the hard, stiff line of his jaw, she could tell that he was clenching his teeth. The muscles near his ear bunched with tension. And his eyes were closed.

That, Rose decided, was the strangest thing of all. His eyes were closed as if he was in pain. Instinctively she placed her hand lightly on his arm.

The moment she touched him, his elbow flexed and his arm jackknifed like he was going to punch somebody.

From sheer surprise, Rose jumped back. "Are you all right?" she yelped.

Skye stared at her one long, disquieting moment. For the first time since he'd walked into her emporium, his eyes brimmed with bald emotion. Finally she could see what he was feeling, and she nearly reeled from the force of the pain.

With visible effort, Skye drew himself together. He looked from Rose to the fist that was still closed. A look of pure self-loathing crawled across his features as he unclenched his fingers and let his arm drop again to his side.

"Are you okay?" Rose queried tentatively.

He flinched at the gently asked question, and once more the door closed on his expression, locking people out, locking despair in.

"I'm sorry I scared you." He rasped the apology.

"Don't apologize." Rose shook her head, amazed. "Not for yourself." She tried another smile. "This will give the regulars something to talk about for weeks. You'll be their local hero. I bet Woody puts it in the *Wiedler Review* when he hears about it."

"No." The single word was short, swift, adamant. "It wasn't entertainment."

"Oh, no, of course not. That's not what I meant at all...."

Skye nodded and ran a hand through his hair.

Rose didn't know what to say. He invited no questions; he offered no explanations.

She couldn't claim to know how a man's mind worked. The little experience she had proved that she didn't understand men well at all, and yet here she stood, feeling the ache in this man's heart as though it were a part of her own soul.

Above all else, Skye Hanks was alone, and that was something Rose understood very well.

How many times this year had she felt the crushing weight of isolation? She could be in a roomful of people and feel like she was adrift at sea, a lonely speck on a wide and endless expanse.

It was an awful feeling, that dismal sensation of being disconnected from the rest of the world when you had no one to tell your secrets to.

Suddenly, with a clarity she felt no need to question, Rose understood that Skye Hanks was more than a prospective date; he was her lifeline to the world of feelings—and she could be his.

"However you feel about what happened here," she began haltingly, "I really appreciate what you did."

Skye said nothing. Rose wound the dish towel around her fingers.

"I won't mention it to anyone if you don't want me to. There's only a couple of people at the counter, and they're not regulars. Anyway, I doubt they heard much."

Skye expelled his breath roughly and nodded. His black hair gleamed in the overhead light. "You think you'll get anyone else at the counter?"

"This afternoon? No." Rose took the opening. "That's what I was saying before. Frank DeRoma wipes us out on Fridays. Sometimes I close early, and—" finding it difficult to make eye contact, she looked down at the twisted towel ''—I thought maybe—''

''I could use the afternoon off.''

The request was clipped and brusque.

She looked up. ''Oh. You mean…starting right now?''

He nodded again. ''Is it a problem?''

He spoke almost without moving his lips, as if every word was an effort, so much like the night he first arrived.

''No. It's not a problem.'' Rose tried to smile.

''Thanks.'' Skye gave a terse nod of his head and moved past her up the aisle.

Even as he walked out the door, she longed to stop him. The bells jingled brightly against the glass, but to Rose, it sounded like a cell door was being slammed shut, locking her once more in a solitary place she'd grown sick of.

# Chapter Five

The school bus cranked to a halt, its large, heavy tires crunching down the gravel road. Most public school buses looked alike, and Skye hadn't paid much attention to any of them since he was a kid.

In fact, he hadn't paid much attention to them then, either. By the age of fifteen, he'd all but quit school, playing hooky most days, finding odd jobs when and where he could.

This afternoon, however, his gaze remained riveted on the yellow bus some fifty feet ahead of his truck. He'd parked neatly along the curb in front of a single-story home set well off the street. He was inconspicuous here.

His run-in with those teenagers at the emporium today had brought back memories, unwanted memories of himself at their age. He knew how easy it was to turn down the wrong road in life, and he wondered if he'd handled the situation well, like Rose said, or if he'd somehow screwed up, added fuel to their fire.

The red Stop arms extended from the school bus, indicating that the children were about to disembark.

Skye straightened against the seat back. One hand tightened on the steering wheel, the other on the photo in his hand. His heart pumped more rapidly than it had when he'd been in the shoot on top of an angry bull.

*Children.*

He wouldn't be a child anymore, not really, Skye thought. This was a high school bus, and the photo he was holding showed a young man, tall for his age, but with a boy's slender build.

The first kids off the bus were three girls, all holding books and with purses slung over their shoulders. Two of the girls crossed the street in front of the bus and one got into a car parked a few yards ahead of Skye. This was a rural area, the dropping-off point for kids who would have to walk or be driven the rest of the way home. He knew that because the information was all there, in the detective's report.

Skye waited. Another kid disembarked. A boy this time... but not the right boy. Impatience, like a hungry wolf, prowled through his veins. Another girl alighted.

He swore.

And then...

"Chad." He said the name softly, as if the boy stepping off the school bus were an infant he didn't want to wake.

Even without the snapshot the detective had sent, he would have known his son. He was sure of it. Same dark, curling hair, same gangly arms and legs that tripped up Skye at that age.

*You'll grow into them,* he reassured him silently, wondering if anyone ever said the words aloud to the kid.

*The kid...*

*My son.*

It was only when he tried to swallow that Skye realized his throat had a lump the size of a fist lodged in it.

His vision blurred. He strained to see as Chad stopped to talk to another teenager who had exited the bus.

According to the P.I. he'd hired to find the boy, Chad would walk this way—right past the truck—then turn left at the corner for the mile walk home. From where Skye was parked, he would get a better-than-bird's-eye view of his son.

The urge to get out of the pickup, ask directions, hear his son speak became so urgent, so overwhelming, Skye gripped the steering wheel and the photo more tightly to keep from acting on the impulse.

Chad lifted a hand and nodded at the boy to whom he'd been talking. He readjusted a green nylon backpack over his right shoulder and started walking toward the pickup.

With each step his son took, Skye felt his heart pound—harder and louder with each pace that brought Chad closer.

Now Skye could see that Chad was a Phoenix Suns fan. He was wearing a Suns T-shirt under the open and flapping button-down shirt that he wore untucked and two sizes too large, in keeping with the current trend. He wondered who had introduced Chad to basketball and whether anyone ever nagged him about his choice in clothing.

A car honked.

Chad drew closer. Skye commanded himself not to stare, but he couldn't help it. He wanted to drink in as much memory as he could. He tensed his arm to keep his hand from moving to the door handle.

"Chad!"

The car honked again. Two short blasts this time, followed by a longer one. "Chad!" The woman's voice was insistent, but not shrill.

Chad looked to his right, smiled, glanced both ways up the street, and crossed to a blue minivan parked along the opposite curb. Skye had not seen the vehicle pull up.

Through the opened window on the driver's side, a blond woman grinned.

It came, then, as Skye had been expecting it to—the rage, as powerful and frightening as the moment he first felt it, the day the detective report arrived and he saw Janet's name listed under "Mother."

For fourteen years he had lived under the cloud of the lie she had told him, that their infant son had been put up for adoption while Skye was in prison. Janet had been only seventeen, two years younger than he, when they'd discovered she was pregnant. Skye had wanted to marry her right away, but Janet's parents had been furious. To this day, he did not know if the decision not to marry him had been Janet's alone or the result of compelling parental pressure. And the decision not to contact him in all these years—whose choice was that?

When he'd first thought of locating his son, all Skye had wanted to do was make sure the boy was happy and well cared for, that the people who'd adopted him were decent and devoted. But not even the resourceful, well-connected private detective he'd hired had been able to find evidence of adoption records. He had, however, found Janet, still living in Arizona.

Her last name was Mason now. She was divorced and had one son—Skye's.

As the blue minivan pulled away from the curb, Skye wrenched his gaze away and turned his head.

He didn't want to think of all the moments he'd missed, all the years he'd spent sitting in a prison cell, never suspecting that she had their son with her all the time. He did not welcome the anger that flared inside him; he didn't want to feel the blame or the rage, but they came anyway, choking him with their intensity.

She had taken away the one thing that might have made a difference in his whole, miserable, lonely life.

"Damn you." Skye's whisper was harsh and awful in its vehemence. "Damn you for damning me."

Rose stared at the copy of *Cosmopolitan* lying open on her lap.

Over the past few months, she had developed the habit of grabbing a magazine off the rack at the emporium and spending an evening scanning the contents for articles about women in the nineties—what they ate, what they wore, what their apartments looked like.

According to the October issue of *Cosmo,* the nineties woman needed gold fishnet stockings to consider her fall wardrobe complete.

Rose sighed. Gold fishnet stockings. Maybe she would get a pair, as long as they came in the support variety for work.

Turning the page, she stared blindly at the next group of pictures.

Her life inched along, and nights were always the worst. Her evenings offered all the variety of a dish of vanilla ice cream: one lick and you knew what you were getting.

There was a knock on her door.

Millard. He'd called earlier and invited her to a bowling tournament—the Wiedler Thunderballs in their much-anticipated rematch against the Sadler Dust Devils. Home alley advantage. She'd declined, but since when did Millard take no for an answer?

Closing the magazine and placing it neatly on the table, Rose stood. Maybe an evening at the bowling alley would perk her up.

Crossing the living room, she reached for the knob and swung open the door. "All right, all right, I'll go." She pushed a grin onto her face.

From the other side of her threshold, Skye Hanks looked at her uncomfortably.

"Hello." His voice was deep and moody.

Rose stared back in surprise. "Hello."

It took her a moment to collect her senses. She stepped back and gestured toward her living room. "Come in."

"No." Skye shifted his weight from one muscular leg to the other, his hands stuffed halfway into the front pockets of his jeans. "I'm sorry, I should have realized you'd have plans."

"Plans?" Rose tried not to babble a denial. Calmly she shook her head. "I don't have plans. Come in."

Skye hesitated a moment, his eyes on her face. Then his gaze shifted past her into the apartment. He moved slowly, and when he stood by the door, just inside her living room, his presence seemed almost massive.

Rose closed the door. "Sit down," she invited. "Can I get you something to drink?"

"Have you had dinner?"

The unexpected question halted her movement. "Dinner? No."

"You mentioned a pizza place."

Her eyes searched his face quizzically. His expression was grim, as was the tone of his voice. He was asking her to dinner, but he didn't look too happy about it.

"Frank's," she supplied the name of the restaurant.

He nodded. His hands were still in his pockets; his big shoulders were hunched. He'd left the emporium more than four hours ago; he looked just as miserable now as he had then.

Rose moved to the chair nearest the sofa and picked up the light sweater she'd draped over its back. Nights could be chilly in the high desert.

"It isn't far from here." She smiled at Skye. "We can walk."

She liked mushrooms and olives and detested pepperoni. Skye knew that because her nose wrinkled when she came across the circles of salami, and she poked them out of her way every time she bit into the pizza. Little piles of pepperoni slices were growing neatly on the edge of her plate.

Skye chased a bite of pizza with a swallow of soda and watched Rose concentrate on cutting a rubbery string of cheese with her teeth.

He'd driven aimlessly for hours this afternoon. His frustration and anger had seemed bottomless and frightening. He'd felt at once desperate and powerless to stem the flow of feelings, and, like most people in pain, he had begun to think that the agony of helpless emotion would go on forever.

And then he had thought of Rose, and comfort.

He was a selfish bastard, he knew. He had hardly said a word since he'd arrived on her doorstep, and he could see how awkward that was for her. But he enjoyed watching her; he felt better, calmer, just having her near.

Turning the glass of soda in clockwise circles, he took a stab at conversation. "We could have ordered it without pepperoni."

Rose looked up from the olive she was trying to nibble off her pizza. She noted Skye's glance at her plate.

"That's all right." She shrugged. "I thought maybe I'd like it this time."

Realizing that for the past several minutes she had been eating merely to fill the awkwardness of inactive silence, Rose pushed her plate to the side of the wooden table. She wiped her mouth with the napkin, smiled nervously at Skye and tried to think of something to say that wouldn't sound like prying. There was so much she wanted to know.

"How long have you run the emporium alone?" He surprised her by initiating the conversation himself.

"A year and a half," she answered. "But I worked it with my grandmother for years."

"Have you lived in Wiedler all your life?"

Rose smiled. After forty-five minutes of silent chewing, suddenly Dan Rather was sitting across from her.

"Yes," she answered, drawing squiggles in the moisture on her soda glass. "That must sound kind of boring to someone who's traveled a lot." She laughed. "It sounds boring to me. I've always wanted to travel, but..."

Skye sat back in his chair and hooked an ankle over his knee. "But what?"

Rose shrugged. "Grandma was older. You know, she needed help around the place...."

She let the words trail off, understanding too well that they held little truth. Lilah would have given her blessings to any adventure her granddaughter had chosen to undertake. It was Rose who had convinced herself she was being dutiful by staying, because she had been too afraid to reach out, too afraid of change.

Somehow the lies that used to comfort tasted bitter now.

Frowning, she amended her explanation. "I'm a creature of habit, I guess. Even when the habit feels more like a rut."

Skye nodded very slowly, his narrowed gaze intent on her face. "Are you in a rut?"

His rich voice was so low and focused, Rose began to feel they were alone, even with the noise swirling around them.

"Yes," she admitted quietly. "I've been in a rut for a very long time."

Skye said nothing, merely gazing at her in that intense, disquieting way.

"Have you traveled a lot?" she asked to fill the silence.

"Enough."

"Did you enjoy it?"

"Sometimes."

The enigmatic answers were not enough for Rose. "What kind of work did you do before you came to Wiedler?" She smiled. "Your application wasn't all that clear."

Skye's expression remained casual as he replied, "I was on the rodeo circuit."

Rose's eyes widened. "Really? What did you do?"

"I rode bulls."

"Bulls?" She leaned forward, eager and amazed. "The bucking kind?"

Skye grinned. "Yeah, the bucking kind."

"Were you good at it?"

"Yes."

Rose looked at him with a question in her eyes. "Flipping hamburgers is a far cry from riding bulls, isn't it?"

Immediately Skye felt his guard go up. She was edging too close to questions he didn't feel ready to answer. Not to her.

Folding his arms across his chest, he gazed at Rose through half-closed lids. "It's a lot safer, though."

Rose rested an elbow on the table and propped her chin on her hand. "Safer," she mused. "I've been safe all my life. I don't think it's all it's cracked up to be."

Frowning, she began to fiddle with the salt shaker.

"How is it you're not married?" Skye asked without preamble, all the more intrigued when Rose fumbled the shaker, spilling salt onto the table. He suppressed a smile when she automatically scooped the white grains into her palm and tossed them over her shoulder.

He might have backed off, realizing that his questions made her uncomfortable. *But,* he told himself, *you're not that nice, so what the hell.*

"*Are* you married?" he rephrased the question, scowling when his thumping heart told him the answer mattered.

Brushing salt from her hands, Rose frowned. "Of course not. You don't see a husband, do you?"

"They aren't always visible. Have you ever been married?"

Her lips in a firm line now, she raised her eyes to his. "Have you?"

"No."

"Have you ever wanted to be?"

Skye hesitated a moment, then answered honestly. "Once. A long time ago."

"Oh."

He waited for her to ask what happened. He wondered if he would tell her.

But Rose didn't ask. Instead, she lowered her eyes, biting the inside of her lip while she thought a moment, then looked up and stated quietly, "I was married once. A long time ago."

It was an offering, not an invitation to further probing, and Skye accepted it as such. But he wanted to know more.

He'd always left other people's private lives alone in the hope that they would return the favor. Now suddenly he wanted to know all about the woman sitting across from him. Who was her ex-husband...someone who still lived in town? Had she loved him? Did she love him still?

Skye stared at Rose and felt an unaccustomed need grow inside him.

Uncertainty and strength—Rose possessed both in equal parts. She was different, completely different from the women he had known during his rodeo days. Willing lips, teased hair, skinny legs in tight jeans—they'd never affected him the way Rose did tonight.

Rose had strong shoulders, broad for a woman, soft breasts and round hips. She had a body a man could rest his soul in.

He wasn't a man who had found much pleasure in one-night stands—relief, occasionally, but never satisfaction. He knew that tonight even physical relief would elude him in a stranger's bed. But with Rose...

She said she'd been married a long time ago. Did she ever—?

Suddenly, strongly, he wished his life were on track and solid, that he had a home and not a motel room to take her to. He wondered if she would go.

A group of raucous teens swarmed the table to the left. Rose glanced over and smiled at greetings from the kids she knew. Skye glanced over, too, then looked back to Rose.

Their eyes met and held, and the rowdy mood of the teenagers seemed intrusive.

"You want to get out of here?" His gaze was hard and his question was searching. He wondered if she knew what he was really asking.

Rose nodded, her expression innocently bland, and together they stood.

As they made their way to the door, several people Skye recognized from the lunch counter called out. He was glad that Rose nodded or said hello in return, but did not stop to chat.

To the right of the door, four old-fashioned pinball machines were in use. At the machine closest to the door, Skye recognized the two would-be shoplifters from this afternoon.

Rose didn't seem to notice, and the young men seemed oblivious to Skye's presence, but seeing them reminded him of the fear and uncertainty in Rose's eyes this afternoon when she'd witnessed his anger.

Leaving the restaurant, they walked into a crisp night. Skye itched to put his arm around her shoulders. *Like a high school kid testing the waters,* he thought cynically, shoving his hands instead into the pockets of his jacket. But as he walked, he wondered what it would be like to escort Miss Rose Honeycutt back to her quaint, single-woman's apartment . . . and then stay there.

## Chapter Six

Rose listened to the muted thud of Skye's bootheels striking the pavement. They walked side by side, she and Skye, her head level with his shoulder, and their arms almost touching.

The night smelled fresh; the stars beamed. In December the storefronts dazzled, with strings of white holiday lights outlining their shapes, but this time of year all was quiet and dark. The shops were closed for the evening, but to Rose the little town had never felt so *alive*.

Sharing a pizza with Skye had proved more exhilarating than riding a Ferris wheel in a high wind.

Once he'd started asking her questions, he'd listened to the answers like she was imparting serious information about the state of the Union. He'd even noticed that she didn't like pepperoni.

And he had the most mysterious, sensual secrets locked in his eyes.

As she walked alongside him, a myriad of possibilities flitted through her mind.

If she were Amy Renlow, she might wiggle her hand into the crook of Skye's arm. She could almost feel the rough texture of his denim jacket as she wondered what his reaction would be.

Keeping pace with his loose, relaxed stride, she unwittingly sighed aloud. It had been a good evening, a *different* evening; she would be foolish and, yes, greedy, to expect more....

Rose took a little forward skip as a broad hand rested on the middle of her back.

Even through her blouse and sweater, his touch sizzled. Breathing harder than their easy walk demanded, she tried to calm her racing mind.

The hand slid up to her nape and squeezed gently.

Swallowing hard, she dared a covert glance at the man by her side. He gazed straight ahead, his expression yielding nothing.

They walked in silence a few more steps. Rose's nervousness mounted until she felt she could not tolerate it, and she began to chatter.

"What did you think of the pizza? Frank has a great sauce recipe. I tried to get him to give it to me once, but he wouldn't. Not that I would have tried it out at the store. I could never compete with Frank, that's why I close early on Saturdays. Frank does a 'to go' business you wouldn't believe."

Skye's hand fell away from her neck.

Rose shut up.

They walked quietly again for several more moments. Then Skye's hand reached for hers. Their palms touched; his fingers closed securely.

Rose's breath caught in her throat. She blinked to clear her vision, but the stars remained a blur through the sweet tears that came to her eyes. She smiled the rest of the way home.

Skye's motel was right across the street from the emporium, but he never even glanced in that direction. He kept hold of her hand and walked with her to the stairs leading to her living quarters.

They reached the foot of the old, heavily painted wooden steps, and Rose's heart began to pound as if she'd run up and down them several times.

He stopped, and she turned, seeking his face in the shadows.

Before she could utter a word to invite him in, Skye raised her hand to his lips. His kiss was gentle and cool, but it burned like a brand.

"Would you...like to come up?" She whispered the words in a daze, wondering vaguely what she had upstairs that would qualify as a nightcap. "I, uh...I have cookies...."

In the light of the full moon, she saw him smile. He shook his head. "Good night, Rose."

He let go of her hand and took a step back.

The pent-up longing inside her screamed that this could not be the end of the evening; it was too soon, and her heart felt too full to end it here. But even as Rose opened her mouth to utter a protest, she saw the curtain of cold distance settle once again over Skye's face.

Mumbling a confused "Good night," she trudged sadly up the stairs to her apartment.

Skye stood where he was, watching Rose until the door clicked behind her and a light went on in the living room. Then, with quiet authority, he spoke into the darkness.

"You boys must have something better to do on a Saturday night." He turned to face two figures hovering in shadows near the corner of the building. "Go do it."

As he spoke, the figures moved closer, coming to a halt just a few feet away. White teeth flashed as the larger of the two boys grinned.

"Now what could be better than catching up with an old friend?"

The boy beside him laughed. "Yeah. We want to further your acquaintanceship, if you know what I mean."

Skye knew. His shoulders tensed and his fists clenched, the physical response to danger swift and automatic. Obviously, his new "friends" were not willing to learn from this afternoon at the emporium.

They were boys, these two hoods who thought it was safe to threaten him because there were two of them and one of him. Damn fools.

Skye had known he and Rose were being followed, and his anger had started mounting almost immediately. He had found a modicum of peace tonight, and it infuriated him to think that these two junior felons were going to try to cause more trouble.

Silently, with the experience of a man used to sizing up opponents, Skye assessed their eagerness to turn this into a physical confrontation.

Hands out of their pockets, arms tensed by their sides, shoulders squared, legs spread—pretty damn eager, he acknowledged, cursing the dark Fates that never left him alone for long.

Once more he tried to send the boys on their way before any real damage was done. "This is a small town, boys. You get into trouble here and it'll dog you for a long time. Trust me. Let it go."

"Gee, thanks for the tip." The larger boy took a step closer. His friend followed. "But we're from Phoenix. That's a nice, large town."

The aggression in his voice was potent. Skye felt a knot of pure, unadulterated rage grow in his gut and pour into his limbs, readying his body for a fight.

They would not heed words; he knew that. They were young, aimless and mean, and they thought they had something to prove because of this afternoon.

He would have liked to maneuver them farther away from Rose's apartment, but they were already taking off their jackets.

Upstairs in her apartment, Rose wandered indecisively. She went into the bedroom to put on a nightgown, then changed her mind, knowing she wouldn't be able to sleep for hours, not with images of Skye Hanks weaving like a carousel round and round in her mind.

What was the matter with her? She had known him such a short while and he wasn't exactly the perfect date, either.

Plopping herself onto a slipcovered easy chair, Rose hugged her arms around her body and mentally ticked off Skye's deficiencies as the ideal eligible bachelor.

*He's closemouthed.*

*Too gruff.*

*His job doesn't pay very well—and she ought to know.*

*It's impossible to tell where you stand with him. One minute he looks as if you're . . . something special . . . the next minute he's walking away and not looking back.*

And yet . . .

Every time she was near him, she felt somehow more *complete* than she had before he arrived. The parts of her that felt unfinished seemed to fill and soften when he looked at her, or when she saw the pain and loneliness in him. He needed her.

Oh, she felt foolish for even thinking it! She had a practical, logical mind, and it told her she couldn't possibly understand the needs of a virtual stranger.

Her impractical, illogical heart, however, told her that Skye Hanks was no stranger; he was the missing part of her.

Restless again, Rose stood and walked to the window. She fingered the heavy, old-fashioned curtains, thinking they really ought to be replaced, then pushed them aside.

Her apartment overlooked the wide, empty alley behind the store. Not much of a view, but she could see the stars, and that went a long way on a quiet evening.

The moon was full and high, lighting the night like a giant street lamp and casting moody shadows on the alley below. There was enough light for Rose to notice movement in the alley.

Pressing her palms against the glass, she inched her face as close to the window as she could and saw three men standing near the foot of her stairs.

*Skye.*

He was down there, but who was with him? The silhouettes of two other men were visible, and something in their stance made the hair on the back of her neck prickle with warning. When the two figures began moving toward Skye, Rose caught her breath in a gasp.

*They're going to fight.*

Even as the thought thundered across her mind, one of the men approaching Skye reared back and swung his fist like a missile aimed at Skye's head.

Rose shrieked, her fingers clutching reflexively at smooth glass as Skye ducked the punch.

She barely had time to register relief before another arm shot out—this time, Skye's. Rose watched, mesmerized, as he grabbed the other man and jerked him close. His right arm arched back, shoulder high, and Rose waited for his fist to crack his attacker full in the face.

The moment never came. Time hung suspended. Skye's fist remained where it was, cocked in preparation for a strike that never materialized. Quickly he had taken the advantage, and just as quickly now, he lost it.

Or rather, Rose realized, watching the scene with mounting dread, he gave it away. Skye stood motionless when he could have struck back. In that timeless moment, he came to some incomprehensible decision.

Releasing his hold on the other man, he let his arm fall to his side and stepped back.

There was no time to hope that a truce had been reached. Recognizing the vulnerability of their prey's position, Skye's attackers seized their opportunity.

The second man, who had been standing to the side, awaiting his turn to fight, leapt forward, grabbing Skye's arm and shoving it up behind his back.

*Oh, stop, stop! You'll break it!* In her mind, Rose cried out, but her fear and anguish were so great the words remained frozen inside her. She could no more move than speak, merely watching the grotesque show as the man Skye had released thanked him by delivering a blow to the midsection that caved Skye in two.

The one holding Skye's right arm, now grabbed his left as well, holding him while the other man prepared to throw a head punch.

Skye straightened.

"Kick him, kick him!" Rose found her voice, though at first it was barely a croak.

*Go for the vulnerables,* her grandmother had always advised on the topic of self-defense. Now Rose saw that Skye had a clear shot at the hoodlum's vulnerables and she willed him to take it.

"No!" she moaned, her heart leaping to her throat as the creep, rather than Skye, again took the advantage. His fist connected in a left to Skye's jaw.

"Oh, what's the matter with him?" Not for an instant did Rose doubt Skye's ability to emerge the victor, even in a two-against-one confrontation. He had strength, he had power; he rode raging bulls. Why wasn't he fighting?

Again the assaulter balled his fist and cocked his arm. This time, Rose did not wait to see the damage done. She flew to the door, wrenched it open and clamored onto the wooden landing, shouting to the ruffians below.

"I've called the police! Get out of here and leave him alone!"

There came an immediate pause in the activity. Three faces turned toward her. Only Skye's looked concerned.

"Get inside." His voice was rough and gravelly.

Illuminated by the light from her apartment, the faces of the assailants were clear now: the same two young men who had tried to shoplift from the emporium this afternoon. They looked meaner and more insolent than before.

Her gaze flicked over them quickly, then returned to Skye. Blood ran from the corner of his mouth. His black hair fell haphazardly across his forehead. She wanted to run to him, to scream the stars down around the heads of these two criminals who had dared to hurt an innocent man.

Caught by the light, Skye's eyes were hard and glittering. Rose read their message clearly, an echo of his raw command: *Get inside.*

Fueled by a sense of outrage that ameliorated her fear, Rose refused to turn away. To her mounting fury, the delinquents paid her little attention. Her appearance did not deter them in the slightest, and her threat about the police made them pause only briefly.

Before Rose could take a single step down the staircase or say another word—before Skye had even turned back to face him—the creep who was doing all the hitting slammed his fist once more into Skye's stomach.

This time, without the glass to muffle it, Rose heard the "oomph" Skye could not contain as the breath was knocked out of him.

Rage, more powerful than anything she had felt before, swelled inside her until she felt like a balloon about to burst.

"Leave...him...*alone!*" Her gutteral cry pulsed against the alley walls. Quickly, with visions of weapons sparking her brain, she dashed back inside her apartment.

Though she had no fireplace, Rose had purchased a set of andirons last winter because she thought they looked cozy in the display at the department store. She grabbed the log poker now, heedless of the other tools she sent crashing to the floor in her haste. Brandishing the iron like a sabre, she charged onto the landing.

"I said, leave him alone!" She snarled the command, failing to notice that Skye had broken free and was standing on his own with his fists raised.

Rose brought the iron crashing down on the rickety railing, splitting it in two with a resounding crack.

She walked down two steps and raised the iron again. "It takes about two minutes for the sheriff to get here from the station. If you don't leave—now—he'll have to call an ambulance."

A pacifist by nature, Rose nonetheless longed to make good on her threat by knocking some sense into the skulls of these two miserable ruffians.

Fortunately she was saved the trouble when a siren wailed in the distance, growing clearer and stronger as the emergency vehicle neared the emporium.

"Go!" Rose roared for good measure, whacking another portion of railing, which also gave way under the force.

Though they were brave in a dark alley, the prospect of a run-in with the local police took the edge off the boys' courage. They cut and ran like champion sprinters.

The siren picked up volume until it was right in front of the emporium, then wailed away into the night. With the fireplace poker clattering alongside her, Rose hurtled down the rest of the steps.

Skye leaned heavily against the railing, his left hand covering his midsection. His head was lowered, but Rose saw the blood smearing his lip and chin.

Tossing her makeshift weapon to the ground, she placed both her hands on Skye's arms. "Are you all right? Did they break anything?"

He shook his head, but his breathing was shallow, as if inhaling more deeply would hurt. His lips quirked in a blood-smeared smile. "That kid can hit."

Stunned by the wry resignation in his voice when she herself still trembled with rage, Rose told Skye exactly what she thought of "that kid."

Grabbing the jacket he'd tossed over the banister, she guided Skye up the stairs, stating with equal clarity what she thought of machismo when he refused at first to lean against her.

They moved heavily but in sync, and Skye wisely chose not to protest when Rose made him sit on her sofa as she went about collecting various first-aid materials.

Returning with cotton swabs, antiseptic, Band-Aids, a bowl of soapy water and ice cubes wrapped in a hand towel, Rose placed the hoard of first-aid gear on the coffee table, then knelt by the sofa. "Where does your stomach hurt?"

Skye looked down at her. "Rose," his voice was raspy and soft, "you don't have to—"

"Hold this against you." She pushed the towel into his hands, then guided his hands to his stomach. "That towel is pretty thick, so it shouldn't get too cold."

Discouraging further protest, she set to work cleaning the blood from his face and disinfecting the cut where his lip had been smashed against a tooth. Skye said nothing while she worked, but his eyes never left her face.

Finally Rose dampened a cotton swab with the antiseptic and attended to the cut on his lip, a rather intimate task for a woman inexperienced in ministering to a man, but she was convinced Skye was too injured to tend to himself.

Using one finger, she pulled his lip down as gently as she could and touched the swab to the cut. His head jerked a tiny bit, but he made no move to stop her.

Kneeling on the floor while he sat on the couch, she met his gaze.

Skye regarded her steadily. He reached for her hand, drawing it away from his mouth. His palm was dry and cool. His long fingers seemed to swallow hers.

Leaning forward, he set her makeshift ice pack on the table, then pulled her up to sit beside him on the couch.

"The police car didn't stop. You never called them, did you?" His voice was tender, almost caressing.

"No. It was a coincidence. I—I think it was an ambulance, actually."

Skye shook his head. "A coincidence," he murmured. Faint humor winked in the depths of his midnight blue eyes. "I've gotten into my fair share of scrapes," he whispered, "but this is the first time I've been rescued by an angel."

He drew her hand toward him. Rose's fingers turned to jelly. She dropped the cotton swab.

When Skye's lips touched her knuckles, dozens of tiny white lights popped and twinkled before her eyes.

"Too brave," he murmured. "If they'd hurt you—"

Anger flared in his eyes, and she shook her head.

"They didn't. Why didn't you fight back?"

As soon as she uttered the question, Rose wondered whether she should retract it. His jaw tensed and his fingers tightened.

"I know you weren't afraid of them," she continued. "You *let* them hit you. I saw you. I know there were two of them, but you could have—"

"What?" Skye's gaze narrowed. "Hit them first? Knocked out a few teeth, broken a jaw? I know how to land a punch that'll do that." His eyes blazed and the grip on her hand became fierce. "What should I have done, Rose?"

He stared at her, beseeching her to understand, and Rose recognized in him the same, smoldering despair she'd seen this afternoon.

"I can take a punch, too."

Rose didn't know what to say. Here was a man with strength and conscience. And if there was danger inside him, there was also compassion and gentleness.

"They shouldn't be allowed to just walk away from this, though," she whispered after a long moment. "We should call the sheriff."

Skye nodded. "But not yet," he whispered back. "In a little while...."

He touched the side of her face. His palm cradled her cheek, her temple. His thumb traced the line of her brow. He touched her like a man drinking from a well, like he was taking something pure, something holy, and his thirst was strong.

"Rose...I wouldn't hurt you, not for anything."

"I know that." Her faith shone in her eyes.

Skye shook his head. "I have no right," he said, but whether he spoke to himself or to her, Rose could not be sure. "No right to want..."

"What?" she asked when he would have let the thought die. This night was for chances. "What do you want?"

He looked at her, and longing quivered in the air between them. "Peace." The hand caressing her cheek moved with aching slowness through her hair. "The peace I feel with you.

"I felt it that first night," he said, "the night you hired me. I felt it when I looked through the glass and saw you light those candles."

Her birthday. Rose felt herself redden, but Skye shook his head. *No embarrassment.*

"Tell me something," he said, and she knew then she would tell him anything, anything at all. "That night...what did you wish for?"

Rose looked in his eyes, tried to memorize the tenderness she saw there. She remembered her wish, its intensity and yearning. "Courage." She smiled. A tiny glowing spot of warmth in her chest took root and began to spread.

"Courage?" Skye regarded her quizzically. "Courage for what?"

"To do this, I think."

# *Chapter Seven*

Like wisps of smoke, her fingers curled into his hair. She did not pull his head toward hers. Rather, she inched up and brought her lips to his.

Skye didn't move at all; he waited. His desire swelled to an aching need that encompassed every part of him—his mind, his body, his soul. And in every way the need felt urgent.

He had so many questions about her, but the first touch of her lips answered the most immediate of them. *Yes*, she wanted exactly what he did.

And *no*, Rose's past marriage had done nothing to dilute her innocence. For one thing, she hadn't learned near enough about kissing.

But Skye could teach her. Starting now.

When Rose's lips sought his, he could feel her careful determination. The first touch was gentle, questing, as if she awaited his approval before carrying on. The kiss was soft and dry, and that wasn't what he wanted, not tonight. Tonight he wanted to taste her, to devour and be devoured, to lose himself and every lousy memory his body stored in the holiness of this one woman's touch.

He lifted his hands, threading his fingers through her hair. He longed to pull her closer. It took every ounce of self-control to do just the opposite.

His muscles tightened as he steeled himself, then pulled away from her searching lips.

Her eyes fluttered open. He held her head and nearly groaned aloud at the sweet uncertainty of her gaze.

"Rose." His voice was thick, hungry. Too hungry. He didn't want to frighten her. "What we're doing here, it's—" His heart thumped and his tongue tripped over the words like a virgin schoolboy's. With a wry shake of his head, he tried again.

"I don't mean to stop at kisses. I want more. I know it's soon." He searched her face, bare inches from his own. "Too damn soon. If you want to stop now, tell me."

In the space of a breath, he saw the uncertainty flare higher in her eyes, then disappear. What replaced it looked like desire and confidence and trust. The trust, more than anything, fueled his hunger and his need, but he had to hear the words that would tell him she knew what she was doing.

"Rose," he tried again. "I barely know you. You don't know me." An understatement. "I know a woman like you expects—"

The fingers that were curled in his hair tightened suddenly. Brown eyes, narrowed and glinting, were as fierce now as they had been gentle and yielding a moment ago.

"You just said you barely know me, so how do you know what I expect?"

Skye frowned. "A woman like you expects—"

*A woman like you...* That was all Rose had to hear to realize she was going to have to *show* Skye Hanks what "a woman like her" wanted.

Convinced he'd been about to say "courtship," Rose wrapped her arms around his neck and jerked him close for a kiss that bore no resemblance to the first. Where the other had been tentative and seeking, this kiss muffled Skye's words and made his brow perspire. Rose had waited long enough for desire to come her way; she didn't want to waste another moment.

At first Skye could do no more than accept the embrace while he worked his way back from surprise. He'd been about to say, "A woman like you expects forever," and he would have added, "I can't give you that," but his words were lost in the unexpected sensuality of her kiss.

Apparently she had more practical experience than he'd first assumed. His senses reeled.

For a man with a fair amount of practical experience himself in matters sexual, Skye was amazed to find that he was trembling.

He brought his arms up behind her back and pressed her body close to his. Acutely aware of her every response, he felt her body tense for an instant, then relax.

They melted toward each other. Nothing, nothing in recent memory had felt this good.

Rose's arms tightened around his neck. Her lips softened and parted beneath his. He nearly groaned.

Hell, nothing in *distant* memory had felt this good, either.

She was different from anyone who had come before; everything about this was different.

He felt her breasts against his chest.

*Real* different.

This was no buckle-seeking rodeo groupie he held in his arms. This was Rose, and when she touched him he knew he had a soul.

Answering the parting of her lips, he moved as carefully as his increasing need would allow.

Holding Rose tightly, he deepened the aching, tender sweetness of her kiss. His tongue skimmed her lips, touching, tasting, finally moving inside. With the first glorious taste of her, he knew one thing with certainty: no matter how near her he got, it would never be close enough.

When Skye's hand caressed her back, Rose thought she might go mad from the sensations swirling inside her.

His kiss…oh, his kiss was something not of this world, not of anything she had known in her world, at any rate. He kissed like he needed her—needed her body, needed her soul.

*I need you, too.*

Her heart spoke back with a yearning so intense, she felt dizzy with it. For so long, she'd felt vacant, like an apartment no one bothered to furnish. Now Skye Hanks had moved in, and if there was a voice inside her whispering, "too soon," there was another voice, coached by years of fruitless longing, that bellowed, "No! Not soon enough!" She'd been waiting all her life to feel this full.

Opening her mouth to his seeking tongue, she answered the question inherent in his touch. *Yes,* she told him with her urgent response, *yes, yes, yes!*

The hand massaging her back moved sinuously to her waist, then higher until his fingers brushed the curve of her breast.

He filled his palm with her, and the heated touch seared her flesh as if her shirt were on fire. When he pulled his mouth away to trail kisses along her jaw and neck, Rose concentrated on every nip of his lips. A feeling like this should be committed to memory.

Skye's left hand slid to her side between her arm and waist, holding her securely while he began very slowly to unfasten the white plastic buttons of her blouse. The little daisies popped free, giving him room to further his exploration.

He brushed his knuckles across the material of her bra. At the first butterfly touch, Rose jumped. He stilled.

Raising his head, Skye took a steadying breath and questioned her in a voice husky with tenuous self-control.

"Do you want me to stop?"

It was in his eyes, in his voice, in the ragged breathing and the pressure of his hand, still heavy on her breast—the last thing he wanted to do was stop.

Rose shook her head, but could not offer the words to reassure him; speech was beyond her.

Taking her chin gently between his thumb and forefinger, he smiled into her flushed face. "You are so lovely."

Lowering his head, he captured her lips with a pressure that was sure and demanding.

How could she doubt the sincerity in his gaze? *So lovely.* No one had ever said that to her before. No one would have made her believe it before.

Gently but with firm insistence, Skye nudged her back until she was reclining against the sofa cushion. He ended the kiss, giving her a brief smile before he turned his attention to the remainder of her buttons.

Rose watched, transfixed, as his large, tanned fingers worked the distinctly feminine buttons free of their holes. At the waistband of her skirt, he paused a moment to tug the blouse free, then continued the unfastening. When she was completely unbuttoned, he pushed the material aside, baring her bra and much of her skin to his gaze.

And gaze he did. He seemed to breathe in the sight of her.

Reaching up, Skye slid one strap of her bra over her shoulder. With a light touch he moved the white cotton cup out of his way and looked at her with infinite tenderness.

Rose shivered.

With his palm cupping her fullness, he lowered his head.

At the first touch of his lips against her bare skin, Rose gasped. She grabbed at Skye's shoulders as he put his mouth around her.

Her head fell back. Ooh, nothing in her life had prepared her for this! Her limited time with Dwyer certainly had not prepared her. Dwyer had touched her, but never like this. Never as Skye was doing right now...with his tongue, so gentle, almost worshipful. Never...oh, good heavens...with his *teeth!*

Rose bit her bottom lip in a desperate attempt to stifle a moan. It was getting harder and harder to take a deep breath.

As his tongue circled her bare flesh, goose bumps shivered across her body, down her legs, along her quivering arms. This time she did moan.

Skye raised his head. Keeping one arm around her back and placing the other beneath her thighs, he lifted her in a single, sweeping motion as he stood from the couch.

The only word he uttered was "Bedroom," and it came out clipped and hard, through a jaw that was nearly locked with tension. Rose took no offense. She could feel the forceful pounding of his heart and knew he was hanging on to his self-control by a hair's breadth. Never in her thirty years had she felt so desired. Never in her thirty years had she desired so strongly.

If there was a moment to turn back, they had already passed it. She was too full of dizzying, mind-fogging sensation to wonder where this step would take them; she knew only that it felt absolutely right.

Burying her face in the curve of Skye's neck, she murmured, "Around the corner, to the left."

She closed her eyes, too choked with anticipation to offer any more directive than that.

Skye moved unfalteringly to the bedroom door, opening it with his shoulder, not bothering with the lights as he found the bed and laid her upon it. He followed her down, his weight pressing her deeper into the soft mattress.

Rose opened her eyes and, in the dim illumination emanating from the living room, watched Skye reach for the buttons of his own shirt. As if she were moving in a dream, she sat up and removed the blouse that was half on, half off her shoulders. Then she reached around and unhooked her bra.

Skye shrugged out of his shirt, but his unabashed eyes never left her as she removed the bra and let it drop off the side of the bed.

Rose's trembling fingers moved to the buttons on the waistband of her skirt.

Skye reached for his belt buckle.

In the shadows, every sound seemed magnified: the click of brass buckle and heavy whoosh of leather. The steely hiss of zipper.

Shaky with anticipation, Rose leaned back, and Skye followed her. Before he finished removing his pants, he continued the exploration he'd started in the living room. Her stomach quivered as his hand reached past the loosened waistband of her skirt to smooth and knead her stomach. What began as relaxing became personal as his fingers sought and found the elastic waist of her panties.

Rose held her breath. Instinctively her legs tensed, and she felt the rough denim covering the masculine thigh that rested between hers. He lowered the underwear past her hips.

Bending over her, Skye whispered raggedly in her ear. "What are you using, sweetheart?"

All Rose heard was the *sweetheart*. Deciding to take some initiative, she stretched up to kiss the hard line of his jaw. One, two, three small kisses.

With a growl, Skye captured her lips, turning her little nips into a deep and smoldering embrace. He finished by tugging on her earlobe with his teeth.

Rose arched against him. Her hands came up to skim across his waist...his ribs...his chest. He was all smooth, lean muscle and taut skin. His flesh tightened in response to her touch, making her feel more powerfully female than ever in her life. His harsh intake of breath added to the dizzying satisfaction.

He spoke against her ear, his voice rusty and strained. "Do you need to get up?"

"Get up?" Rose murmured, confused. Why would she get up when she was finally right where she wanted to be?

She traced an imaginary line from his armpit to his waist, letting her fingernails draw another growl from him. "No," she answered dreamily.

Skye sat up, his smile just visible in the darkness. "This needs to come off."

Exerting admirable control over his impatient hands, he removed her skirt, then stood briefly to divest himself of his jeans. He returned to the bed, bracing himself above her.

Rose gasped as his hands found her buttocks. He pressed her firmly, intimately against him.

"You never answered me," Skye reminded her.

Rose was breathless. "Answered you?"

Her heart pounded wildly at the sheer solid maleness of him. If they stayed together fifty years, if she lived to be a hundred, she would never take this for granted. Never, never, never!

"So." She felt Skye's grin against her ear. "What kind of protection are we using here? I think I should know, don't you? And tell me fast, because I'm losing the war with self-control."

Rose frowned. *Protection.* For a moment she couldn't marry the word to its pertinent meaning. But then . . .

*Birth control?*

"I . . . I . . . oh." Her eyes widened in surprise and dismay. "I haven't, uh . . . I wasn't exactly . . . we aren't using any."

Delivering a wobbly smile against his neck, she realized that she hadn't thought about birth control in—oh, for goodness' sake, she'd never thought about it. With her husband, she'd been perfectly willing to start a family. Since then, she'd had no need for birth control, and with Skye . . .

With Skye, everything had come as a surprise—the passion, the urgency, the very fact of him. At the age of thirty, Rose Honeycutt had been married, but she had never really had a lover.

Now the lover in question pushed himself up on his arms to stare down at her.

The tension radiating from him made Rose feel suddenly that she was in the path of a volcano about to erupt.

When she stirred beneath him, Skye snapped, "Don't move," in a tone not very loverlike.

He remained absolutely still for several long moments. The effort seemed to command all his concentration. Finally he expelled a protracted, shuddering breath and moved off the bed.

An excruciating silence followed as he donned his jeans and rammed his arms through his shirtsleeves. Rose felt paralytic in the face of his anger, but when he buckled his belt and leaned over the bed, she nearly jumped.

"What the hell kind of game do you think you're playing?"

"G-game?"

"I asked you—twice," he growled, "what kind of birth control you were using. If I hadn't asked you again, I never would have gotten an answer, would I?"

Vibrating with barely contained rage, he moved away from the bed and raked a hand through his hair. "How the hell can a woman your age hop into bed without thinking about the consequences?"

"I— My age?"

Skye shot her an insinuating glare. "You're old enough to know better, sweetheart."

*Sweetheart* sounded far less like an endearment than it had the first time he'd said it.

Rose yanked the bedspread around her. "Now wait a minute—"

"*You* wait a minute. Maybe you like playing Russian roulette with your life, but I don't, and I don't want anyone else putting a gun to my head."

"A gun to your head?" Jerking the covers to her neck, Rose sat up. "What is that supposed to mean?"

"It means," Skye began in a snarl, then stopped abruptly and paced away from the bed.

The light from the living room cast him in silhouette with his back to her, his hands on his hips. Shaking his head, he expelled a breath that sounded more like a hiss than a sigh.

"It means we *both* made a big mistake." His tone was gritty and tired. "And I'm too damn old for mistakes."

Before she could think of how to respond to that, Skye was out of the room. She heard him move through the living room, pause a moment, then open and close the door.

Rose sat on the bed, feeling shell-shocked. For the life of her, she couldn't think of what to do. Cry? Scream? Run to the door and scream at *him?*

In moments of confusion, Rose's grandmother used to say, "Just do what's in front of you."

In front of Rose were her clothes—the ones Skye had removed—scattered on the carpeted floor. Reaching over to snap on the bedside lamp, she let the light chase the shadows away.

A moment ago her bedroom had been filled with magic and mystery and wonder. Hard to believe that scant minutes ago her soul had felt so full that she didn't think her body could hold it.

*Just do what's in front of you.*

Dragging the bedclothes with her, Rose gathered the garments and hurled them into the tidy closet.

"Stupid!" she cursed herself. "Stupid, stupid, stupid!"

How could she have acted so precipitously? She was the type of woman who spent days debating the pros and cons of switching toothpastes. Tonight, reason had flown out the window, and to what end?

Grabbing her robe from the closet, she slipped it on and trudged morosely into the bathroom.

When she flicked on the light and looked into the mirror, however, Rose saw something that transformed shame and humiliation into a far more constructive emotion.

That was no embarrassed little girl staring back at her. Her mirror reflected a woman, one who had tasted passion. And she wasn't sorry; she was angry!

Rose pounded her fist on the tiled sink. Yes, she felt anger, a roiling, satisfying anger at that big...cowboy...*jerk!*

She'd made a mistake, yes, but what about *his* responsibility? What about staying and talking if there was a problem and working it through? He'd bolted the moment their physical relationship was no longer a possibility.

So maybe all he'd ever wanted was a little fun, and when that was no longer possible, there was no reason, as he saw it, to stay.

Reaching for a brush, Rose spent some of her increasing outrage on an aggressive attack of her scalp.

After a few strong strokes, she lowered the brush and shook her head. No. One week, one month, or one year, she knew him well enough to know that wasn't the truth. They had both acted irresponsibly, and he had *re*acted very badly. That was the truth.

"I'm too old for mistakes," he'd said. Well, he'd better have been talking about the situation and not her. She was not a mistake!

Regardless of how he had perceived it, Rose had seen tonight as a beginning. She had waited nearly half her lifetime to know what passion was. From the moment she first saw him, she felt Skye Hanks was her destiny.

Sighing, she raised the brush and pulled it through her hair again, this time more kindly.

"Destiny," she murmured sadly.

So, what now? Back to the emporium in the morning. Back to days that bled into each other with nothing to distinguish one from the next. She closed her eyes against the realization that she had dreamed of going away with Skye when he left. "Two drifters, off to see the world," just like in the song.

Emotion squeezed her chest. Her throat began to burn, and the longer she stood there refusing to cry, the sharper the feeling became.

All she could do was pray that Monday at the emporium Skye Hanks would quit, so she wouldn't have to fire him. Because what she absolutely could not do was go to work every day staring in the face of a future that would never be hers.

# Chapter Eight

The emporium was closed on Sundays.

The first thing Rose felt when she opened her eyes was gratitude for her one-day reprieve. With luck, the only thing she would have to face today were the dustballs behind her refrigerator.

Rolling over, she squinted at her clock and groaned. Eight a.m. With all the tossing and turning she'd done, she hadn't slept more than four hours. Shmooshing her pillow until it was a satisfying ball, she flopped onto her stomach and tried to go back to sleep, but her eyes refused to stay closed.

Someone was sawing outside her apartment.

At least, the metallic whine that grew more insistent by the second sounded like sawing.

Throwing off the covers, Rose straightened the zip-up robe she'd fallen asleep in, shoved her feet into slippers and went to investigate. Her alley was usually so peaceful, especially on Sundays, when most of Wiedler was quiet as a ghost town.

When she opened her front door, sunlight blinded her tired eyes for a moment, and she blinked to adjust to the light.

The sawing stopped. From the porch, she looked down into the alley. Skye stood at the foot of her stairs, looking up at her. He had one hand on a plank of wood that was hanging off the bed of his pickup and the other hand curled around the grip of a large saw.

He wore the same cowboy hat he had on the night he first came into the store and a light blue cotton shirt with the sleeves rolled up. She didn't want to think about how good he looked, so she concentrated on the solemn expression freezing his features. Stone Man was back.

"Morning." His lips barely moved when he spoke. He nodded once.

*If he calls me ma'am, I'll throw my slipper at him,* Rose decided while she waited for him to offer some explanation.

He stared at her a while longer. "Did I wake you?"

She chose not to answer that, gesturing instead toward the wood. "What are you doing?"

Skye looked up from beneath his Stetson, glad of the brim that shadowed his face. Politeness dictated that he take the hat off or at least nudge the brim back so the person he was speaking to could see his eyes, but it was easier this way. He felt like the lowest form of life after last night. He was furious with himself.

Last night, he'd blamed Rose for something that was as much his fault as hers—more his, really, because upon reflection he realized that her eagerness was a product of need, not experience. When he remembered the trust in her gentle brown eyes, he felt like a fist was driving into his stomach.

He was known on the rodeo circuit as "Suicide" Hanks. He had ridden the meanest bulls, hung on the longest time, taken chances he didn't have to take to win. His willingness to self-destruct had bordered on the legendary, or the insane. But nothing he had ever done on the circuit felt as self-punishing as what he did last night.

Lousing things up with Rose was like cutting off his own supply of oxygen.

*Say you're sorry, Suicide.*

Yeah, apologizing would be a decent start. But what if she didn't want to forgive him?

Worse still, what if she did?

He had no business attempting a relationship with a woman like her, a woman he could hurt. A woman who needed a hell of a lot more than a fly-by-night could give. He had no experience in loving, at least not for long.

*Say goodbye, Suicide.*

Do the lady a favor. Don't apologize, don't make her forgive you. Don't hang on to a bittersweet dream. Just take care of your business and get the hell out of here.

"I came by to fix your railing." He didn't have to remind her he was the reason she'd broken it. She nodded. "If it's too early—"

"No." She shook her head, a tiny movement as tense as her expression. "Thanks."

He couldn't summon another word and yet he felt the strangest sensation: the *desire* to speak, something he almost never felt. For an instant, just an instant, he wanted to tell her about everything—his son, his past, all the godforsaken pain. He wanted so damn badly to tell her he was sorry about last night and that he was sick of being alone.

The need to talk to her stunned him with its force and swiftness, leaving him frightened...and more silent than before.

He wasn't sure whether Rose said anything else before she turned and went back into the apartment, but he was aware of the cold sweat that broke out above his upper lip and brow.

In her apartment, Rose sat on her sofa, went to the kitchen, opened the refrigerator, shut it, walked back into the living room, straightened the coffee table and sat again. She leaned back against the cushions, but couldn't relax. When she started to rise once more, she knew she would never be able to stay in this apartment while Skye was right outside.

She had to talk to someone.

A glance at the clock discouraged her, but only temporarily. Eight-fifteen on a Sunday morning would find Millard in church, snoozing through the sermon while he waited for the pancake breakfast that followed the service. She could either wait at his apartment or intercept him before he got to the pancakes.

Dressing quickly in her customary jeans, blouse and sneakers, Rose grabbed her purse and car keys and indulged in a little clear lip gloss for her descent down the stairway.

In the end she decided to wait at Mill's apartment. Showing up at church to waylay her friend would cause too many questions.

Ten o'clock had come and gone by the time Mill ambled up the walkway.

"You have a little maple syrup there on your suspenders," Rose greeted him, changing the surprise on his face to a frown as he looked down and located the sticky spot.

"Well, shee-oot. How does that happen?" He licked his thumb and rubbed at the stain. "What are you doin' over here this morning?" he asked before looking up again.

Rose shifted. Now that she was here, she worried about how Mill would respond to what she was going to tell him.

He looked like a cross between Albert Einstein and Santa Claus, a fuzzy Yogi bear of a man who was as dear as he was wise.

"I miss Grandma," Rose surprised herself by saying.

Mill studied her a moment with that wonderful amalgam of gentle shrewdness in his faded blue eyes, then nodded and opened his apartment, motioning her inside.

Rose entered and seated herself comfortably on the battered sofa Mill had been planning to upholster for the past fifteen years. She waited while he went to the kitchen, got a paper towel and returned to the living room, rubbing ineffectually at his suspender.

"I was thinking of Lilah, too, this morning," he said.

"You were?"

"Yup. Pastor Jack got to talking about carrying each other's burdens and whatnot, and I got to thinking about your grandma."

He caught the flash of surprise Rose couldn't quite conceal and grinned. "Now, don't go lookin' at me like that. Just 'cause my eyes is closed don't mean I ain't hearin'."

Rose smiled. "Grandma told me once that in all the years she knew you, you'd never let her down."

"Nah," Mill dismissed this with a gruff wave of his hand. "We all let each other down at one time or another. But Lilah was the best friend I ever had." He glanced up from under his brows and pointed a finger at her. "Don't tell Ray. He says he thinks we're like Butch and Sundance. Butch and Sundance! Now ain't that a crock?" He shook his head. "Ray's gone a little soft in the noggin since his wife died. I don't like to hurt his feelings."

"I won't say anything."

Giving up on the stain, Mill balled the paper towel and tossed it into a large, flat ashtray Rose remembered seeing at the senior center's last yard sale.

"What is it about Lilah you're missing this morning?" he asked, leaning back in his reclining chair until the foot rest popped up.

Rose smiled at the comfortable picture he made. She shrugged. "I miss the way she listened. Like she was hugging you with her eyes. I miss talking to her."

"And what is it you're needing to tell her?"

Rose swallowed hard. She had no idea how Lilah would have responded to what she was going to say. And no idea how Mill was going to react, either. "I want to sell the emporium."

Mill showed remarkably little emotion of any kind. When he pursed his lips, his chin wrinkled, but that was about it.

Rose felt a disturbing combination of nervousness and irritation that her bombshell had so little immediate fallout. "Aren't you going to say anything?"

"I think you better begin at the beginning."

He listened without interruption—and without judgment—as she told him about her attraction to Skye Hanks and about the events of last night. Stumbling over her words, she forced herself to be honest about her confusion and embarrassment and, prior to those feelings, her eagerness.

"I mean, I must need a change if I was willing to...to...you know, be *close*...to someone I barely know." Her face flooded with color. "I'm sorry, Mill, am I making you horribly uncomfortable?"

"Darlin', I got two well-grown kids, five grandkids and over forty years of ranching under my belt. I ain't the one blushing."

Rose buried her hot face in her hands. "But *me! Me,* Mill. I don't do things like that! I can't imagine what Grandma would say."

Mill considered this thoughtfully. "Rosalie," he said after a time, "your grandmother would be shoutin' hosannas that you're finally over that good-for-nothing dust spider ex-husband of yours. *Dwyer.*" He said the name like he was swallowing cod liver oil. "Lilah never worried about your morals, honey. She worried that you'd got yourself too hurt to take a chance again. And a good life—" he shook his head "—it's nothin' but chances. That's all she ever wanted for you. A good life."

"Chances," Rose mused, shaking her head. "Grandma used to read me fairy tales. I liked 'Sleeping Beauty' the best. She didn't have to get dressed and go to a ball. She didn't have to find her way home or figure out how to turn straw into gold—she just ate an apple and took a nice, long nap. And when she woke up, the prince was there."

Mill grunted. "Sounds dull."

Rose nodded emphatically. "I know, that's what I liked about it! No risks. I used to think Sleeping Beauty was so incredibly lucky, because all she had to do was go to sleep and wait for life to come to her."

"And what do you think now?"

Rose gave the question due consideration. "You snooze, you lose." She leaned forward like a child with a new idea. "Oh, Mill, there are so many things in life I've never even dared to want. I'm afraid to waste any more time."

"What do you want?"

That question was harder to answer. She struggled with the possibilities for several long moments, then shrugged and expelled a long, frustrated sigh. "I'm still not sure."

"Hard to find something when you don't know what it looks like."

"Are you saying I shouldn't sell?"

"Nope. That's your decision. All I'm saying is when you don't know what you're running to, you can wake up one morning and realize that all you've done is run away."

Frustration gripped her more tightly than ever before. "If I'm running away, at least I'm *moving* for a change! And, anyway, what is there to run away from? I have a decent life, a nice life, but there's no...passion. There are only so many ways to cook hamburger and plenty of people who can do it just fine."

She stood and paced the narrow living room. "Well, I'm tired of *decent* and *nice* and *just fine*. I want *extraordinary...wonderful*. I want to do just one great thing. I want to *feel* one great thing." She shook her head, looking down at her hands. "Just once I'd like to know that I've made someone feel something only I could make them feel."

"You've done that," Mill stated firmly, "for your grandma, for me, for lots of folks."

She looked at Mill, plaintive in her need for understanding. "I want more."

He nodded slowly. "Still, it seems to me you're looking for a someone, not a something."

Resuming her seat on the couch, Rose rubbed her hands across her knees. "Maybe, but someones are hard to find."

"Yup. But it could take a while to sell the emporium, too. Not a whole lot of people movin' into Wiedler. What'll you do in the meantime?"

"I don't know. Plan, I guess. Decide where I want to go first. I'll miss you, Mill."

He smiled gently. "I'll miss you, too, but you ain't gone yet. First things first. What are you gonna do about last night?"

"What do you mean?" Rose wanted to talk about moving away and changing her life and creating a new identity, not about dealing with dashed hopes and abject humiliation. "There's nothing to do. He ran out last night and barely said three words to me this morning. I made a mistake. I almost made a huge mistake. As far as I'm concerned last night was just proof positive that I need a change."

Mill pressed the footrest down with his heels. The chair tilted forward. He sat up and pursed his lips thoughtfully. "But it's unfinished. You just going to ignore what happened? Go on working with him like you're nothing but boss and employee?" He made a clucking sound out of the side of his mouth. "I don't see how you're going to do it."

"He doesn't seem to have a problem with it."

Millard accounted himself a good judge of character. He found it hard to believe that Skye, whom he'd judged to be decent and honest, if a little closemouthed, could turn out to be so callous when it came to Rosie's feelings.

To Rose Millard answered, "The point is, do you have a problem with it? Just 'cause someone ain't in a talkin' mood, don't mean you gotta shut up, too."

Rose shook her head stubbornly. "He was a mistake. Talking about something that's clearly over and done with would be too humiliating. I just hope he'll quit."

Mill quirked a bushy brow, and Rose held up a hand to forestall any further comment. "I know, I know. I need to act, not react. But if I fire him, I could be sued for sexual harassment."

A wide grin split Mill's face. "Well, now, that would be different." He enjoyed her discomfort for a moment, then asked, "You want a soda?"

"Sure."

"Top shelf of the refrigerator. Pour me half a glass with ice." He continued to smile blandly while Rose dutifully got up to get the soda, but the wheels of his meddlesome old mind started turning the moment she was out of the room.

When Skye opened the door to his motel room later that afternoon, Millard was the last person he expected to see. The old man appeared even more gruff and full of spit and vinegar than usual as he eyeballed Skye from head to toe, then barked out a question that sounded like an order.

"You play pool?"

"What?" Skye hadn't even had time to summon a hello.

"Pool!" the old codger repeated as if Skye were deaf or stupid. "Eight ball. Do...you...play?"

Skye leaned against the doorjamb with his arms crossed and took his time answering. "I've played once or twice."

"Okay." Millard nodded slowly, his eyes narrowed and loaded with speculation. "Let's go."

They walked to a bar three blocks from the motel, both men silent all the way. Skye was a bit surprised to find a bar open and busy in the small town on a Sunday, and he saw immediately that it was the type of place he disliked: dark and full of smoke and so run-down it appeared seedy. Still, he knew they hadn't come for the ambience—or the pool. Millard wanted something, and Skye was curious enough to go along for the ride.

When Millard gestured to the rack of cue sticks, Skye walked over and made his selection.

Mill slapped the rack onto the felt table and snapped, "Rack 'em!"

Stifling a smile, Skye once again obliged. Not bothering with the niceties of who invited whom, Mill stepped up to the table and broke first.

He sank three balls, then missed the four and stood back with the fire of challenge gleaming in his eyes. "Your turn."

Skye tried to put the four ball in a corner pocket on the head rail, but missed and consequently set up a clean shot for his opponent.

"Not too good at this, are you, boy?"

Skye remained noncommittal.

Mill sank the four, chalked his stick and scratched on a shot that should have been easy, leaving Skye with another opening.

When Skye capitalized on his chance, sinking a ball in each side pocket, Mill decided it was time for an additional challenge.

"You a gambling man?" he asked, leaning on his stick.

"That depends," Skye answered, wondering with some amusement whether he was about to be hustled. "What are the stakes?"

"Words, son. The stakes are words. If I win, I get to ask you a question, any question I want, and you gotta answer it."

"What kind of stakes are those?" At the moment, Skye found himself more plainly surprised than intrigued.

"I'm on social security, son, I don't play for money, anymore. But I'll buy you a beer if you win."

On the rodeo circuit, Skye had gambled with his very safety time and again. Somehow the stakes seemed more daunting today, but curiosity won in the end.

"All right," he agreed and sank one more ball before Millard trounced him soundly, never again giving him the chance to catch up.

Being a good sport, Mill sprang for two beers and waited until they were seated in a dingy but private corner of the bar before asking his question.

"What were you in prison for?"

The old man's expression remained as placid as a summer's eve. Skye had to struggle to keep his own features a neutral mask. Before he decided how to reply, Millard offered a sketchy explanation.

"Scooter Nelson did some time a while back. He saw you in the store the first day you worked, but didn't want to upset Rose in case you hadn't told her, so he came to me. I watch out for Rosie. I'm the nearest thing she's got to family."

Skye nodded his acknowledgement of the proudly issued warning, feeling his respect for Millard mount. "She's lucky." Raising the draft beer, he took a sip, using his lower lip to blot the foam. "I don't remember a Scooter Nelson."

"He was John Nelson back then. We call him Scooter 'cause he moves like he's on wheels."

"Mmm." Skye couldn't remember a John Nelson, either, but he guessed it didn't matter. The past caught up whether you moved like you were "on wheels" or not. "Didn't John Scooter Nelson tell you what I was in for?"

"Said he didn't remember ever knowing. Said you kept mostly to yourself."

"That sounds about right."

The two men watched each other for several long moments. Skye had lied by omission on his job application, and it didn't sit well with him. How many times in the past had reporters dug up the information that he had done time? It was a matter of public record, but Skye had never felt an obligation to answer their questions. His life was his business; they could judge him on his present conduct or not at all.

And yet, since coming to Wiedler and searching for Chad, past and present had merged. Seeing his son for the first time and meeting Rose had awakened needs that went beyond having a decent place to live and a regular paycheck. It was precisely that—his new vision of a better life, a richer life—that made his past seem more damning than ever. He wanted more now than he'd dared to hope for before, and that wanting gave birth to fears of judgment and condemnation for who he'd been and what he'd done.

When he looked at Millard, he wanted not to escape the truth, but to put an end to the bittersweet longing. A glimmer of disgust or fear on the old man's face might convince him once and for all that dreams of home and family were wasted on him; he hadn't belonged to anyone, or they to him, since he was twelve years old.

"Manslaughter." He answered Millard's original question with a single, taut word, allowing the abruptness of his tone to indicate there would be no additional explanation.

The old man watched him closely, his expression betraying nothing.

"How long were you in prison for?"

Skye took another swallow of beer. "One question. You already asked it."

Mill smiled. "I did, didn't I?" He raised his own glass in a genial salute. "Guess that'll have to satisfy me."

Skye couldn't believe what he was hearing, or seeing. Mill raised the glass, drank some beer, then started speaking generally about the various pool tournaments he'd participated in and about a hustler named Vernon "The Eight Ball" Heyer, who drank whiskey through a straw and taught Mill everything he knew.

No disgust, no fear, not a single grimace crossed the old man's face in response to Skye's revelation. He merely chatted amiably, exuding—and seeming to invite—genuine friendliness.

Skye felt an odd, uncomfortable sense of being in limbo. Where was the irrefutable proof that dreams of home and family and place had no business lodging in his heart? Millard claimed to be Rose Honeycutt's great protector, yet here he sat, friendly as an eight-week-old puppy.

"Manslaughter means I killed someone," Skye surprised himself by pursuing the issue.

"Yeah, that's what it means," Mill agreed, sobering respectfully. "'Course it also means someone in charge thought you didn't mean to do it." He scratched the

stubble on his chin. "Unless you plea-bargained down
from a murder charge or something of that nature." His
clever eyes narrowed. "Did you plea-bargain, boy?"

"No."

"Huh." They sat in silence for a few moments, then,
"Who'd you kill, a man or a woman?"

This time Skye answered immediately. "A man."

"Was it an accident?"

"I'm not sure that matters," Skye said, his voice low
and heavy. "I didn't want to kill him. I did want to hurt
him."

"You figure wanting to hurt someone is as bad as
wanting to kill him?"

"Given the outcome, it was."

Mill nodded. "Well, son, I figure you're right. I guess
you've paid for it, though."

Skye released a snort of disgust. "How do you pay for
someone's life?"

In that moment, Mill understood that Skye had, in one
way or another, been paying for years, even to the point
of refusing to defend himself in an unequal fight. He
thought about Rosie's account of the disastrous evening.

Skye, Mill decided, was a responsible man. He kept
himself solidly in check, which was why Mill was beginning to believe that his feelings for Rosie were genuine,
and that they extended beyond the physical. It made
sense. A man like Skye—self-condemning, wary and
honest—could do a lot worse than a woman like Rose—
straightforward, caring, and ready to take a risk.

"You planning on stickin' around?"

To his credit, Skye answered this, too, with candor. "I
don't know."

Mill nodded. "Okay." He drained his beer. "C'mon, let's play another game." He stood and ambled from the table.

Skye stared after him.

No opinions, no suspicion, no suggestion that Rose was off limits, or should be.

He shook his head. Mill had left all the decisions—and the judgments—up to him.

Closing his eyes, he allowed a small, ironic smile to play about his lips. He didn't know whether to feel vindicated or damned.

# Chapter Nine

Monday's breakfast special was a chorizo omelet.

Normally Millard loved the Mexican sausage and all the other ingredients Rose threw in; he liked to think of this breakfast as his spicy wake-up call for the week.

Well, either he was getting old or Rose was having a bad day again, because there wasn't enough water in all of Wiedler to put out the fire roaring in his gut, to say nothing of the inferno in his mouth.

Gamely he tried another bite from an innocent-looking corner of egg. He nearly choked.

"What's the matter?" Scowling heavily, Rose turned from where she was hacking into a slab of bacon. She held a meat cleaver in her right hand.

Mill looked at her with watery eyes. "Nothing."

On either side of him, the other Monday-morning regulars coughed and sputtered.

"Well, you all sound like you have consumption,"

Rose grumbled, turning back to the bacon and taking an unnecessarily nasty pass at it with the cleaver.

Beside Millard, poor Ray took a bite of the omelet Rose had recently set in front of him. His thin shoulders shook as he coughed. "This ain't natural," he gasped. "I gotta order somethin' else."

"Shh. No you ain't," Mill hissed out of the side of his mouth. He didn't want Rose upset any further; she could poison the whole town.

"But, Mill," Ray whined, "I'm hungry!"

"Shh. Shut up and eat."

Rose heard the mumbling behind her, but chose to ignore it. She had a horrible headache. Tossing and turning all night, she had finally arisen at four this morning, after only a couple hours of sleep. Skye had called at seven to tell her—without explanation—that he was going to be late. Now she wished she'd just stayed in bed.

All night and well into the wee hours of the morning, she'd worried about her decision to sell the emporium. True, her dissatisfaction with her life had been growing for months, but was this the answer?

As she fell asleep last night, she tried to imagine what her life would be like when she was free, no ties to bind her to anyplace or anyone. That's when the insomnia had started.

The bells on the front door heralded a new arrival. Disciplining herself firmly, Rose refused to turn around to see if it was Skye. She stayed where she was, chopping the bacon into chunks for split pea soup.

"Morning!"

"Morning!"

The cheery voices of the Renlow twins rang out over the coughing at the counter.

Rose tried very hard not to groan. Annie and Amy Renlow never came to her counter in the morning. Rumor had it that no one had ever seen them in the hours before noon.

"Hi, Rose!" Amy trilled as she slid her voluptuous body onto a stool. "Where's that cute helper of yours?"

Turning to face the fully coiffed, painted and tightly garbed twins, Rose gritted her teeth. "He's not here yet. Is there anything I can do for you?"

"Oh, you see? I told you it was too early to come here," Annie said around a disgruntled yawn. "Let's go."

"Hush." Amy swatted her sister's arm. "We heard something real interesting last night at the Chomp 'N' Stomp." She named a restaurant and country dance club on the outskirts of town.

"Oh, yeah?" Rose set the cleaver down and wiped her hands on the towel she'd tucked into her apron. "What's that?"

Amy leaned onto the counter, serving up a lovely view of her well-exposed cleavage. "Do you know what your helper did before he came here?"

"Hey, Rosie, can I get some more coffee?" Mill called loudly from his place several seats away.

"Sure, Mill, just a sec. Of course I know," Rose answered Amy. "He was a bull rider in the rodeo."

Amy smiled knowingly. "That's not all."

"Rose, Ray could use another biscuit." Millard held up a hand, pointing to his friend's plate.

"'Kay, I'll be right there," Rose promised distractedly, hooked into the conversation, despite herself. "What do you mean, that's not all?"

Annie yawned again, then graciously accepted the piece of toast offered to her by the customer on her left.

Amy, however, had interests more pressing than sleep or food. "He's not just any bull rider," she announced, looking as pleased as a Hollywood columnist with a fresh piece of gossip. "He's Suicide Hanks."

"'Suicide'." Rose frowned. "What are you talking about?"

"Rockin' John, the bartender down at the Stomp, likes the rodeo. He was in here Saturday and said he couldn't believe his eyes when he saw Suicide Hanks flipping burgers. That cowboy of yours has ridden some of the nastiest bulls this side of the ever after. He's practically famous. R.J. says he wouldn't let go until it looked like every bone in his body was busted. That's why they called him Suicide. He was meaner and crazier than the bulls!"

Amy appeared to be thrilled by that last idea. Even her sister perked up as she heard the story repeated. "He's won more buckles than any rider in the last ten years," Annie added around a mouthful of buttered toast.

*Suicide Hanks. A rodeo star.*

Amy voiced Rose's next thought. "What's he doing *here?*"

"Hey!" Mill barked, leaning forward to glare at Amy. "There's nothing wrong with this place. If you don't like it—"

"Oh, I didn't mean anything bad," Amy said with a charming smile. "I just mean, why work as a fry cook when you've traveled all over the country, winning rodeos? He must be starving for a little excitement." Amy and her sister exchanged glances fraught with meaning.

"Aw, he's excited enough," Mill countered gruffly.

Rose appreciated the staunch defense, but privately she concurred with the Misses Renlow. She knew just enough about rodeos to know that men who'd won a number of buckles could boast a number of groupies, as well. And

to think that Skye had garnered more buckles than anyone in the past ten years! Amy was right. Skye must be
bored out of his mind here.

And Saturday night...

Suddenly Rose felt a powerful need to lock herself
somewhere very dark. Why was it that wanting someone
could make you behave so stupidly? Her inexperience
must have seemed so obvious, so pathetic to him. No
wonder he'd expected her to be prepared; he was used to
women who had as much experience as he did.

Thank heavens they'd stopped when they had! A few
more moments of unearthly sensation and she might have
blurted something really humiliating, like "I love you."

She wanted to throw her apron over her head and sob
when she realized that for him Saturday night amounted
to little more than another form of recreation.

"How 'bout some of that coffee, honey?"

Swimming laboriously back to the present, Rose saw
that Mill was eyeballing her with concern. "Sure, Mill.
Sorry." She dredged up a limp smile and took the cof-
feepot to his place on the counter.

Steam swirled from the cup as she poured. Mill
touched her arm. "Don't pay any attention to them," he
whispered gruffly. "That boy's happy here."

Rose almost laughed. She nodded, refilled Ray's cup,
too, and turned away.

Sparky Owens took a seat at the counter and Rose
busied herself with his order. She knew when Skye arrived because Amy Renlow stretched the words "Well,
hello" into ten syllables.

Not to be outdone, Annie swallowed the last of the
toast she'd filched and purred, "My, Mr. Hanks, morn-
ings certainly are picturesque around here since you
showed up. You're a fine-looking man to have breakfast

with." She giggled as if she could hardly imagine a shy creature like herself uttering anything so bold. "I hope you don't mind my saying so?"

Rose stood in front of the griddle with her back to the counter and squelched a longing to turn and slap Annie with the spatula.

Skye offered a courteous, "Thank you. That's kind of you."

Rose noted Skye's approach from the corner of her eye. "You're late." Her voice was nowhere near as silky as Annie Renlow's. Still without looking at him, she stacked three flapjacks onto a plate.

"I told you I was going to be late."

In no mood to be charitable, Rose grumbled, "I know, but . . . you're later than you said you would be."

It wasn't true, but he didn't bother to point it out.

Plopping a little scoop of butter onto the pancakes, Rose grabbed a maple syrup and carried it to Sparky. He smiled the big, toothy, thank-you grin he'd smiled every morning for the past dozen years.

She watched him pour the syrup in ever-tightening circles over the round cakes. He started on the edges and moved in toward the center, just like he always did. Then he took his fork and swirled the butter into the syrup. . . same as usual.

Rose stared, feeling like she was stuck on the "repeat" cycle of a time machine. Giving herself a mental nudge, she moved to get Sparky's coffee.

Amy Renlow wiggled on the counter stool and dimpled sexily at Skye. "What's good to eat today? I always wake up *hungry*."

That did it. Something broke free inside of Rose. The safety catch on her personality snapped. She sashayed over to Sparky and dribbled coffee into his mug—his customary half cup with the first pancake. Smiling broadly, she used one finger to scoot the mug closer to his plate, then leaned her hip against the counter.

"There you go-o." Her voice oozed like honey on warm bread. "What else can I get you, *sugar?*"

Sparky lifted his attention from his plate. "Sugar?" He blinked dumbly. "Naw, no thanks, Rose. Just black, like usual." He lifted the mug and blew on the steam.

Rose stomped to the coffee machine and slammed the pot onto the burner.

When Amy ordered a chorizo omelet made extra hot by Skye's "very own hands," Rose figured she'd suffered enough. Avoiding Mill's astute gaze, she left the counter, grabbed a feather duster and retired to the canned goods aisle.

Dusting the tops of the canned lima beans, she sighed. She wasn't cut out for romance in the nineties. Not that she'd done too well in the eighties, either.

She had no idea how to flirt, and she didn't have a casual bone in her body. Skye had seen her *naked*, for heaven's sake; in her book, they should be married by now, not flirting with other people!

Distracted by her thoughts, she dusted the green beans three times before she realized what she was doing. Moving on to another group of cans, she nearly jumped when Skye spoke from right next to her.

"Customers are all taken care of for now," he told her, jerking a thumb over his shoulder to indicate the counter. "Mind if I talk to you for a minute?"

"No." Rose reached up to turn a can of sliced beets so the label faced out. "I don't mind. Go ahead."

He began awkwardly, "Listen, about the other night—"

Rose felt her whole body tense.

"I'm sorry," he said. "It shouldn't have happened."

*Which part of it?* Rose yearned to ask, but she didn't dare. If he said he was sorry about all of it, she would never be able to look at him again.

She made an inarticulate sound of dismissal. "Don't be silly. It was just one night. We got a little carried away and didn't think." Mustering every ounce of fortitude, she faced him with a bright, wide smile. "Don't worry about it, no one got hurt."

He grunted. "Look," he persisted, "I said some things I shouldn't have—"

"Really? When?" Rose asked ingenuously.

"When? When the hell... After... You know when!"

Rose affected a puzzled frown. "Oh, you mean when you realized we'd forgotten a method of protection?" She actually sounded nonchalant.

"Yes, then."

"Pfff." She waved a hand in dismissal. "I can't tell you how relieved I am that you kept your head."

"Relieved," he repeated, his hands going to his hips as he stared at her. "You are, huh?"

"Yes." She nodded emphatically. "It was a very emotional night, what with the fight and all, but thank goodness one of us had some presence of mind. When I think of the deep and lasting regret we'd be feeling now if you hadn't kept your cool—"

"Deep and lasting—" A horrible scowl darkened Skye's brow. "Look, don't say anything else for a minute, okay?"

"Fine!" Rose crossed her arms and waited for him to continue.

"I'm trying to apologize," Skye sighed. "I implied that you were irresponsible. That you do that kind of thing all the time." He shook his head, and the irritation on his face was replaced by an expression of extreme gentleness. "And I know that isn't true."

"Well, hardly." Rose sent him a look of shy disbelief, while inside she seethed.

The nerve of him. Condescending rat! Insensitive lout! Who needed one's ex-would-be lover to point out that one's inexperience was obvious?

Hiding her fury behind a smile, she elaborated. "Saturday night was *very* different for me," she agreed.

He nodded. "I know."

"Yes. After all, I've never been intimate with a rodeo star before."

A sudden stillness came over him. "Rodeo star?" he repeated tightly.

Rose flicked the feather duster over the cans. She shrugged. "Word gets around, *Suicide.*"

When he grabbed her arm, his grip was mercilessly strong. "What the hell are you talking about?"

"Nothing you haven't heard before, I'm sure. A man's occupation can be a lure in itself." Vaguely, Rose was amazed by her own behavior. "Let go of my arm."

Looking down as if he hadn't realized he'd grabbed her, Skye immediately loosened his grip.

Rose straightened her blouse. "What I'm saying," she began calmly, now wanting only to end this conversation, "is that you don't have to worry about leaving hurt feelings behind, okay? What happened ... almost happened ... wasn't about feelings, was it?"

Skye looked at her a long time. His face reflected a myriad of emotions: surprise and anger, acceptance and then a cynicism she hadn't seen before. His mouth lifted at one corner.

"What was it about, do you think?"

Nervous under his scrutiny, she shrugged. "Fun, I suppose. What do you think?"

"I think we were robbed."

His hands shot out so quickly, she didn't have time to be surprised. Skye dragged her against his chest and lowered his head, pausing when there was only a breath's worth of space between their faces.

Letting go of her arm, he brought his hand up to cup the back of her head, his long, hungry fingers twisting through her hair. His mouth came down on hers, claiming a kiss that was nothing like the others they'd shared. This one was neither seductive nor giving. This one took and branded and made certain she would remember the man as well as the kiss.

He raised his head and slowly his fingers slid through her hair. Letting his hand fall to his side, he took a single step back.

He stared at her a hard moment, until Rose became aware that the rhythm of his breathing matched the rapid beat of her own heart. Then, like melting butter, his lips spread into a slow, liquid smile. He cocked a finger at her, level with her trembling mouth.

"Now *that*," he said, "was fun."

Turning almost before she had a chance to register the words, he sauntered away.

Rose scurried to the end of the aisle in time to see him resume his position behind the counter. He retied the apron he'd earlier discarded and smiled at the Renlow twins, who were still working on their breakfasts.

"How are those omelets, ladies?" His voice was smooth as scotch whiskey. "Hot enough for you?"

Above their twittering heads, he met Rose's gaze, straight on.

# Chapter Ten

*P*ick up the phone.

Skye sat on the rough, worn-out bedspread in his motel room and stared at the beige phone on the nightstand, an amenity for which he paid extra. Unconsciously his fingers flexed, clenched and flexed again. He'd been sitting here like this for fifteen minutes. Outside, afternoon had yielded to evening.

Impatient, frustrated and scared, he ran his hands through his hair and swore at himself.

"You've been a lot of things in your life, but you've never been a coward." *At least, never before.*

He swore again. Life was easier before, when he'd been content to be alone. Now he had a need to get his life on track, and the challenges were daunting.

Like picking up that phone and calling Janet.

He'd tried to call her this morning and had wound up sitting on this bed, staring at the wall for twenty minutes before he gave up and went to work.

When he'd first arrived in Wiedler, he'd thought it might be enough simply to see Chad, to know he was safe and cared for and content. He would check on his boy and then leave, and if he took with him renewed pain and fresh anger over all he'd missed . . . well, he could handle that. Those were feelings he was used to, and the ones you were used to seemed natural, even strangely comforting, after a while.

But there was Rose.

Being with Rose offered the promise of a different kind of comfort. A comfort that was pure and simple, one he could feel down to his very bones. A comfort that would take away the pain, if he let it. . . .

If he wanted Rose, he had to put his life in order. He had to believe a man could begin again.

*Pick up the phone.*

The number he needed was on a piece of wrinkled white paper he'd been carrying in his wallet. It was lying unfolded and smoothed out on the nightstand now.

Palms that stayed dry in his gloves even when he was sitting atop a bull the size of a pickup truck were now moist with perspiration. He reached for the phone, cursed when his finger shook, punched out the number. She would be home. He knew their schedules; the private detective had drawn it all out. Chad had baseball practice till six, but Janet would be home. If they were following their usual schedules, her parents could be home, too.

He willed Janet to pick up the phone herself.

Ring . . . ring . . . ring—

"Hello?"

Her voice was still high and sweet. For an instant he felt trapped once more beneath the angst of a kid from the wrong side of the tracks, calling Janet at home, when he knew her parents would hate it.

To steady himself he took a deep breath he hoped she couldn't hear. "Janet . . . this is Skye."

Rose walked behind Walt Pettifor as he paced the aisles of her emporium, clucking, grunting and making notes to himself on his chipped brown clipboard.

"You'll have to get me a complete list of your inventory, of course," he mumbled with his chin down toward his chest, the clipboard resting against his soft stomach as he scribbled.

"All right," Rose answered. She'd called the real estate office that morning and scheduled the appointment with Mr. Pettifor.

"There's no mortgage, and that's good. No liens or other claims against the store or anything in it?"

"No. Nothing." Her grandmother had left it to her free and clear, and that was how she'd kept it. She took some pride in that.

"You collect any rent for that unit upstairs?" He pointed to the ceiling with his pen.

"No, that's where I live."

He blinked behind the heavy frames of his glasses. "Oh. Right. Fine. Shouldn't be too hard to rent out. Extra income potential." He committed this last bit of information to paper, then looked up. "Are you hoping to live here when the building sells?"

Uncertainty squeezed Rose's chest. Where was the spirit of change that had fueled the phone call this morning? It was too soon for seller's remorse.

Lifting her chin like Joan of Arc on the stake, she stated calmly, "No. I won't be living here after it sells."

Mr. Pettifor's pen moved again, and Rose had to squelch the sudden weakness that made her want to cry out, "Don't write that down!"

She plodded behind the real estate agent as he examined the kitchen equipment. She could barely mask her relief when he clicked the pen, stabbed it back into the breast pocket of his mustard yellow shirt, and announced that he'd seen everything he needed to see for now.

"Drop that inventory off as soon as you can, and we'll decide on a price for the business."

"Yes, all right." Feeling slightly queasy, Rose followed him to the door.

She opened it and Mr. Pettifor stepped out.

"Excuse me." He made a funny little hop to his left to avoid bumping into Skye, who moved aside and let the Realtor pass by.

Skye remained where he was, just outside the door, until Mr. Pettifor got into his economy-size hatchback and drove away.

Night had fallen and somewhere close by a cricket chirped insistently. Rose knew she would find it in the store tomorrow if she didn't close the door. She was always finding crickets in the store. . . .

"Can I come in?"

An hour and a half ago, he'd left smelling like hamburgers. Now he smelled fresh, like her soap aisle.

Rose stood immobile. She'd barely spoken to him after that . . . kiss . . . that . . . that . . . *devouring* . . . earlier in the day. She hadn't thought about it again, either.

Not much.

Leaning against the cool glass, with the string of bells pressing into her hip and thigh, Rose tried hard not to stare—or even glance—at his mouth.

"What are you doing back?" she asked the lines on his forehead. "Did you forget something?"

"Can I come in?" he repeated.

She flipped a hand into the store, and Skye walked past her. Letting the door sway shut, she turned and trained her gaze on his neck, anywhere but his mouth.

Discomfort hunched the line of his shoulders, tensed his neck muscles.

"Listen," he began awkwardly, much as he had when he apologized earlier in the day, "about this morning—"

*"Don't...you...dare!"* Her eyes shot to his face. "If you apologize again, if you *dare* say you're sorry you kissed me, so help me, Skye Hanks..."

"So help you, what?"

Puffing heavily, she growled through gritted teeth. "So help me, I'll fire your butt right out of here!"

Skye nodded, digesting her threat. "You think I'm sorry I kissed you?"

"You were about to apologize for it, weren't you?"

"Hell, no!" Skye denied, hands on his hips. "I'm not going to apologize for that. Kissing you is about the only thing I've felt really good about in a helluva long time."

He made his declaration without looking away, his blue eyes steady and intent.

He took a step toward her. "I'm not sorry I kissed you," he reiterated, and Rose felt the edges of her vision fall away until all she saw was Skye. "I'm sorry for the way I kissed you. And for what I said afterward." His mouth quirked. "It was a damn sight more than fun."

"It was?"

He nodded. "I was angry when I said we both got cheated the other night. I was angry when I kissed you."

Regret carved lines around his mouth. "That's not how I wanted it to be."

Rose felt the information zoom past her like tiny whizzing jets. Suddenly there was so much to hang on to: he'd been angry, now he wasn't; their kisses meant something to him, something more than recreation, and *he wanted to kiss her again*.

She didn't know what to respond to first.

"Why were you angry?" she asked in a hushed tone, the only volume she could manage.

Skye took a deep, ragged breath. "This morning, you, ah... You said emotion had nothing to do with Saturday night." He shook his head. "I didn't like that. I've been with some women in my time, Rose—"

"How many?" she blurted, then colored immediately, appalled by her temerity.

He smiled crookedly. "Somewhere between more-than-I-should-have and not-as-many-as-you-think. Most of the time I didn't care if all a woman wanted was a rodeo buckle or just a little fun with someone who wouldn't give her any trouble afterward, who wouldn't make any demands. It didn't matter, because it was easier that way. But that wasn't what was going on Saturday night. Nothing is easy with you."

Closing his eyes, he expelled a short, harsh breath. "I'm not good at this. I don't have the words." Opening his eyes, he looked at her with a wealth of emotion. "I'm not good at talking about...feelings. But I know they were there Saturday night. For me. And it scared the crap out of me. Then when you said it wasn't about emotion for you, for a while there I believed it."

"Now you don't?"

"No."

"Good." She met his gaze, full of regret and even shame that she had lied about her feelings to protect her dignity.

It was what he already knew, or he wouldn't be here. He had seen through her lie because he understood; he knew what it meant to care—or to want to care—so much that fear began to overwhelm need. He understood the relentless ache of rejection.

Rose felt it again, then: the dizzying rush of awareness, the sensation that she was at last connected to another soul. In that moment, when she saw his vulnerability, too, fear receded and the truth—speaking it—seemed important.

"When you left Saturday night, I was so embarrassed. Ashamed. I thought I must have seemed so inexperienced and naive—"

"No," he interrupted swiftly. "I was wrong. Being prepared wasn't only your responsibility."

"I know that." Rose smiled. "But the fact of the matter is I *am* inexperienced. When the heat of the moment was gone, I felt foolish. Then Annie and Amy Renlow came in this morning and told everyone how famous you were, and . . ." She shrugged dolefully.

Nervously locking her hands, Rose tried to make sense of her fears. "I was married for eight weeks. Dwyer, my husband, didn't like to work. He thought the emporium brought in a lot more money than it does, and he figured I'd own it someday when my grandmother died."

The frown on Skye's brow grew deeper with each word she spoke. Rose forced herself to push on.

"When he realized my grandmother intended to make him work for his keep and that there wasn't a lot of extra money to throw around, he decided to head out and look for greener pastures—with a cocktail waitress from Flagstaff.''

Rose smiled as if, by now, the memory were nothing more than an anecdote, but the pain of such a callous betrayal ran deep, and Skye was not fooled.

"What the hell did you see in the bastard?" He didn't bother to soften the sentiment.

"He liked me," Rose said with heart-wrenching simplicity. "Or he seemed to. I went through an awkward phase when I was growing up." She mustered a rueful smile. "It lasted fifteen years. I didn't think I could be the type of woman that men find attractive, so I didn't try. And then Dwyer asked me to marry him, and I was so happy, I didn't bother to wonder if I loved him."

At that moment Skye wanted to smash Dwyer and every other blind idiot who had ever looked at Rose without really seeing her.

What Skye saw was a woman rich in experience that had nothing to do with how many men she'd known, and everything to do with how deeply she'd felt in her life. He saw beauty and a combination of shyness and poise that was poignant and lovely in its very contradiction.

He saw yearning and willingness and an understanding of how precious a relationship could be.

He saw all that and he wanted it for his own.

He was a selfish son-of-a-gun. He'd been alone so long, he wasn't sure he knew how to be anything but selfish. It scared him. Most people had at least one relationship they could point to with satisfaction and say, "There, for that person at that time, I came through. I was what he needed. I didn't let him down."

There was no one about whom Skye could say that. Only two people had ever needed him, truly needed him—his mother and his son—and he'd failed them both.

God, if he got involved with Rose he would let her down, too. Would she hate him then? Would she see the void, the gaping, nameless deficiency that kept him always a step away from feeling whole. *He let people down.*

The urge to run slammed through his body, fast and overwhelming. He fought it like an alcoholic wrestling with the need for a drink.

He felt the sudden desire to pray, to cry out to the Maker he'd long ago given up on, for guidance or instruction or maybe salvation. But as quickly as the desire came, an awareness settled upon him.

Salvation, if it were possible for Skye Hanks, was staring him right in the face.

"Rose." Her name rolled from his lips like a benediction. He stepped forward with a hand raised, intending to touch her cheek, but he curled his fingers into his palm and let his arm drop before the contact was made.

"Rose." His voice was gravel rough. "There are things about me you need to know. Things I ought to tell you right now, but, damn me, I don't want to. Not tonight."

She held him with her eyes like a child holding a brand-new toy—greedy and full of wonder.

"I want to stay with you tonight," he whispered. "Above the covers."

Her confused expression was almost comical. "You mean . . . just sleep?"

He allowed a smile to curve his lips. "There may be a certain amount of kissing involved. All right?"

She said nothing; she didn't even smile, but her face changed. She glowed from within, like she had a wonderful secret. When she held out her hand, her movement was slow and languid, but there was nothing tentative about it. Skye reached out and clasped her fingers; they curled gently around his. The sweetness shot straight up his arm.

They walked in silence out of the store and up to her apartment, and for the first time in years Skye was content to follow someone else's lead.

For the first time ever, Rose was content to take it.

It was only when they reached her living room, Rose faltered a bit, wondering what she should do.

It was still the middle of the evening. She could take him into the kitchen; he might be hungry. Turning toward him, she began, "Are you..."

His eyes were loitering on her face, giving the distinct impression he'd been staring at her all the way from the emporium. He wanted to stay with her tonight, perhaps just to hold her. Tonight she had something to give.

When was the last time she had felt a man's strong arms around her? Had she ever?

She never completed her question. She didn't have to.

With Skye in tow, Rose moved directly to the bedroom. When she got there, she didn't waste time wondering what she *should* do. For once, she did as she pleased.

Letting go of his hand, she crossed to the walnut dresser against the wall and bent to open the lowest drawer. It took her a moment to find what she wanted, an ivory satin nightgown with ribbon drawstrings at the low-cut neck and the waist: the sum total of her trousseau.

Eight years ago, on her wedding night, her brand-new husband's lack of interest had made wearing the gown seem frivolous. Afraid of feeling foolish, she hadn't even bothered to put it on for him. She knew that tonight there would be no such worries. The gown was just clothing, and clothing couldn't make her any more or less special than Skye already found her.

And he did think she was someone special. It shone through his smile when she turned back to him.

"I'll be a few minutes." Her customary shyness mingled with tingling anticipation and an exhilarating sense of boldness as she retired to the bathroom.

She emerged shortly thereafter, feeling more shy and less bold in the flowing, feminine night attire. It only took one look at Skye, however, for her focus to shift from herself to him.

He was lying on the bed—above the sheets, as promised—with only his jeans to cover him.

Of course, they covered quite a bit of him, but what they left exposed . . . Oh, glory. . . .

Rose stood on the threshold of her bedroom and stared. No, that wasn't quite true. She didn't stare, she *savored*. His arms were crossed beneath his head, and his eyes were closed. She took the opportunity and the time to drink him in like wine and breath. All the strong, male power of him. To wake up to that every day . . . the muscle, the strength, the heart . . . to sleep beside him every night . . . to cherish, even when he was no longer by her side, the knowledge that they were never really apart. . . . That was what she wanted.

Skye's lightly furred chest lifted and fell subtly. Moving carefully in case he was asleep, Rose crossed to the empty side of the bed and got in. As a matter of habit, she slid underneath the covers. When she reached up to turn off the light, the room plunged into a darkness that seemed to increase the silence and the intimacy.

Drawing the covers beneath her arms, Rose stared at the ceiling. She could pray all night for the courage to touch him, but that would be asking too much of herself. She closed her eyes.

"Are you going to fall asleep?"

Pitched low, the masculine voice sounded like it was right in her ear.

Her eyes flashed open. "I thought *you* were asleep."

Skye rolled onto his side, propping his head in his hand. "I cheated. I wanted you to feel relaxed." He paused and she heard his breathing in the silent night. "Are you relaxed?"

"Oh, yes." Her voice squeaked. She felt Skye smile.

"Me, neither." Another pause. "I can't remember the last time I held someone in bed. Or out of it."

Rose turned her had. "Really? You? I thought you—"

"That's not the same thing."

They stared at each other, their eyes gradually adjusting to the darkness.

Rose spoke quietly. "I haven't been in bed—for any reason—with anybody since Dwyer."

"Why not?"

She thought about it a long time. "I always think it's because nobody's asked, but I guess the truth is I've been afraid."

Gently, he reached out to brush a forefinger down her cheek. "He was a horse's ass," Skye whispered, brushing his thumb along the corner of her mouth when she smiled. "Do you want to try it now? See how it feels?"

She knew what he meant and nodded.

"Roll onto your other side."

Rose turned over with her back to Skye. His arm came around her, circling the area between her navel and breasts. He drew her tightly toward him, her back coming up flush against his chest with only the sheet and the thin material of her nightgown separating them.

When his chin came to rest in the curve of her shoulder and neck, Rose was sure she had died and floated to heaven. And heaven was warm.

She let her arm rest gently atop his and closed her eyes.

"Rose?"

His whisper sent goose bumps shivering down her back.

"Hmm?"

"It feels," he said, referring to the simple act of holding each other, "damn good."

# Chapter Eleven

Wrapping a thin, motel-issue towel around his waist, Skye stepped from the shower and let his mind wander lazily over the past twelve or so hours.

A smile began deep in his chest and molded his lips. Damn, it had been a fine day.

He'd left Rose's apartment in the early hours of the morning, while she was still asleep. It had seemed right that way. He thought she would be more comfortable preparing for work as she usually did.

Now that he thought about it, everything about the day had progressed as it usually did: customers came and customers went; he grilled hamburgers, and Rose blended shakes; she chatted with the friends she had known all her life, and he let the comfortable patter soothe him like a good massage.

Nothing out of the ordinary.

And nothing quite the same.

Leaving the bathroom, Skye walked across the nubby brown carpeting and noticed for the first time the way it felt against his bare feet. Why was it that every fibrous material in cheap motels felt like it needed a good sanding? Rough towels, rough blanket, rough carpet.

Rough life—drifting from city to city and room to room.

Ah, but today... Today, every move felt purposeful. He could ride a bull for eight seconds and walk away before a cheering crowd, wondering what the hell the point was. This morning all Rose had to do was smile and he felt like flipping pancakes was a holy mission.

Everything had changed. Even the way he felt about this meeting with Janet.

Pulling a pair of trousers and a dress shirt from a garment bag, Skye dressed with care.

He had told Rose he would see her later tonight. He hadn't told her about Janet yet, but he would then. He would explain everything tonight.

Slipping a tie beneath the collar of his shirt, he realized that his meeting with Janet, even telling Rose the truth about himself, seemed less intimidating than it would have only twenty-four hours ago. Trusting someone colored every action.

As he left his room at the Good-Night Motel and got into the cab of his truck, Skye took a long look at the Wiedler Country Emporium and Café. For once, courage seemed to come from someplace other than inside himself; it was a relief. For once, there was someone to come back to.

The Cantina Roja was dark and quiet, which was probably the reason Janet had chosen it as their meeting place, that and the fact the restaurant was located in

Flagstaff, far enough away to make running into anyone she knew unlikely.

Skye sat with a basket of broken tortilla chips, a monkey dish of watery salsa and a club soda on the table in front of him.

At three minutes past five, Janet walked in.

He had already seen her through the window of her van the day she'd picked up Chad from school. So it came as no surprise that she was still beautiful, but he found it interesting to note that she'd dressed much as he had, eschewing jeans for a more conservative pants suit.

He debated standing as she approached the booth, but the tight expression on her stunning face stopped him. Clearly even in this obscure place, she wanted to attract as little attention as possible.

Sliding into the booth, she placed her purse on the seat next to her, adjusted her jacket and drew her arms in close to her sides before looking at him.

"Hello, Janet."

"Skye." As a contrast to years ago, the breathiness in her voice sounded as if it came from stress rather than flirtatiousness. "You look good." Her eyes flicked over his shirt and tie. "Different, but easy to recognize...."

Her voice trailed off, as if she realized that neither of them cared a fig anymore about the other person's appearance.

"Thank you for coming," Skye offered into the silence.

"I'm not sure I had a choice."

A waitress dressed in unflattering orange and yellow flounces approached the table.

"Would you like a drink?" Skye asked.

"What are you having?" Janet pointed a slender, French-manicured finger at his glass.

"Soda."

Her lips curved in a wry challenge. "As I recall, it used to be rum and cola."

"For both of us," Skye agreed, remembering too well the clandestine drinking of their youth.

Janet conceded the point. She nodded toward his drink and addressed the waitress. "I'll have the same."

Turning back to Skye, she came right to the point. "How did you find me?"

Skye considered the wording of her question somewhat ironic. "I wasn't looking for you," he told her quietly, without rancor. "I hired a private detective to find Chad."

Neither of them could ignore the wealth of implication behind his words. They both knew he'd expected to find his son living with adoptive parents, not with the mother who had said she was giving him up.

"Why did you look for him?" Janet's well-shaped brows furrowed above her hazel eyes. "Why now?"

Skye felt his jaw clench. *Why the hell not?* he wanted to shout from his side of the table. *He's my son.* Controlling himself with effort, he modulated his voice. "If I'd known you had him, I would have looked for him right away. I thought he was with strangers. I didn't want to disrupt his life, but I reached the point where I needed to make sure he was okay."

After a taut silence, Janet ventured in a strained voice, "You'd be disrupting his life now."

She looked so miserable and so afraid, Skye almost felt sorry for her. Almost.

The waitress brought Janet's soda and asked if they wanted to order food. They passed.

Leaning forward with his forearms resting on the table, Skye tried to keep the anger out of his hushed question. He was only partly successful. "Why, Janet? Why lie to me? Why let me think he belonged to someone else all these years? I had a right to know."

"You didn't!" Her light eyes flashed with their first spark of temper. "You were going to prison, Skye. I had to think of my baby—"

"And yourself."

"Yes, and myself! What kind of life would we have had waiting for you to be free? And how would anything have changed when you got out of prison? You looked for trouble. You were so reckless."

"Just one of the charms that drew you to me, as I recall," Skye pointed out cynically.

"That's true," she agreed without resentment. "I'd lived such a pristine, sheltered existence. Daughter of the town mayor. I thought I was the world's biggest bore. And there you were. And everything you did was outside the rules. Being with you made me feel like a rebel. But that was kid stuff, Skye. A temporary rebellion."

She drew her club soda closer and poked a fingernail at an ice cube, frowning heavily. "For you, trouble was a way of life. When I decided to keep the baby, my parents' values didn't seem so silly, anymore." She looked up, entreating him to understand. "Every child deserves stability in his life. You couldn't have given that to Chad."

"I never got the chance."

"No one forced you to fight. You could have walked away."

Janet spoke softly, almost reluctantly, but her words fell like knives as Skye remembered the altercation that changed his life forever—and ended another man's.

"There is no way to explain to a young child that his father is in prison. And I had no way of knowing what you'd be like when you got out, no reason to believe you could put aside your anger and your self-destructiveness and be there for us."

For a brief moment, Skye closed his eyes and felt it all again: rage, impotent frustration, the endless, bottomless agony of failure.

Guilt swelled inside him.

"What have you told him about me?"

Janet's gaze shifted uncomfortably. "I told him his father was young, which was true, and that he wasn't ready for the responsibility of a family. I got married when Chad was three. His stepfather was very good to him, Skye. We're divorced now, but they still see each other every weekend."

His stepfather. Skye knew he should feel grateful, but it wasn't in him; not yet. At least Chad knew he had a father out there somewhere. That should make things easier....

"I want to see him." His voice was hard, flat, final.

One look at Janet's face made it clear that this was what she feared most.

"Skye," she reached a hand blindly across the table, "you can't. The divorce shook him up. He got into some trouble for a while. Nothing serious, not drugs or anything like that. But he was acting out—in class, at home. He's finally settling down. Don't bring more chaos into his life."

"What makes you think that's what I'd bring? Chaos." Because he didn't want to prove her right, Skye kept his anger in check. "He's my son. We have a right to know each other."

"You want to tell a fifteen-year-old boy that you were in prison?" Janet's tone assumed a new hardness. "You want to explain *why* you were there? He'll think it's romantic. It'll be a license for him to get in trouble so he can be just like his dad."

"You're not giving him much credit for common sense."

"Common sense has nothing to do with being fifteen! This isn't about what you want. This is about what's best for Chad. That's how you raise children."

Her hazel eyes narrowed and the lips he remembered as sensuous thinned into a tight, desperate line. "I've worked hard to create stability for him, to steer him away from the problems his generation can get lost in. I've given him the kind of head start a child deserves ... *and I will not let you dance in and screw it up!*"

"Don't tell me what you will and will not do, Janet. You've been calling the shots for fifteen years. That's long enough."

Hanging on to his temper by a thread, Skye took out his wallet, threw down the money for the drinks and a sizable tip, and stood.

"I'll call you," he growled, and if she took it more as a threat than a promise, he didn't care.

Barely conscious of anything outside the thundering in his ears, Skye left the restaurant and the mother of his only child without a backward glance.

*The sun's rays spread like melting butter over the day, coating everything in a hazy, golden glow.*

*It crossed Skye's twelve-year-old mind that if he was going to steal, he ought to be doing it at night, but then he decided he wasn't really stealing, he was borrowing. And, anyway, flowers grew back.*

*Mrs. Clarke had a whole garden full of flowers, more than just one person could water, probably, and he only needed a few of them, just enough to make a nice bunch for the vase his mother kept on the dining room table.*

*Twisting the stalk of a tall orange flower whose petals looked like the crepe paper he used in art class, Skye felt the sadness and sharp ping of fear that always came now when he thought of his mother.*

*He hated to remember the look on her face when she came outside last week and saw that he'd forgotten again to water the primroses she'd planted outside the door of their apartment. The flowers' pink and white faces were drooped over like they'd surrendered to an evil enemy. His mother hadn't said anything, but her face had looked so sad. That was how she looked all the time now...sad, or like she had a terrible stomach ache.*

*He hated it.*

*He ripped another flower off its stem, taking less care this time, and laid it on the ground with the others he'd picked.*

*His mother hadn't come outside again since that day. She hardly ever left her room lately. They never ate dinner together anymore, either. Neighbors brought in food, but he ate it by himself on the coffee table in front of the TV. He wondered if Mrs. Clarke would stop bringing casseroles when she saw what he'd done to her flowers.*

*What Skye hated most of all, though, since his mother had gotten sick, were the sounds. The nighttime sounds. He heard the low moans, like someone was being hurt in her room, and no matter how much she smiled at him when he went in to see her the next morning, he couldn't forget the sounds.*

*Why hadn't he watered her flowers?*

*Scooping up the blooms he'd filched, he started back to the apartment, hoping he'd gotten her favorite colors and trying to picture her the way she used to look when he'd come home from school and she'd be on her knees patting the dirt around her plants with soft, loving hands. She did everything like that—soft.*

*Eager now to see her response when he brought her the vase filled with the bouquet, Skye raced the rest of the way home. The flowers would make her feel better, he knew. They always did.*

*Turning the doorknob, he used his shoulder to push the cheap wood panel past the point where it always got stuck and raced into the dining room. He grabbed the vase off the table, took it to the kitchen and stuck it under the tap, his enthusiasm growing by the minute.*

*Shoving the stems into the water, he turned to leave the kitchen.*

*"Skye, is that you?"*

*Mrs. Rusillo, who lived in the apartment right next to theirs, called out from the living room. Mrs. Rusillo came over a lot lately.*

*Skye felt a moment's irritation. He wanted it to be just him and his mom when he gave her her gift.*

*Mrs. Rusillo met him in the dining room. She was a small woman with plump arms and a plump neck and a big, baggy chin like a pelican. Whenever Skye saw her, she was wearing an apron.*

*He spared her a quick smile. "Hi, Mrs. Rusillo. Thanks for the meat loaf. I had it last night. I gotta go give these to my mom."*

*"Skye?" Her chubby fingers reached for his arm before he could move past her. "Darling, your mother—"*

*"Let go, Mrs. Rusillo." Chubby or not, her fingers pinched his skin.*

*He looked toward the hall leading to his mother's bedroom. A woman in a white uniform with a starched cap emerged, closing the door behind* **her**. *Skye thought* *the cap was the ugliest thing he'd ever seen; it was so huge, it seemed to take over the woman's head.*

*"I want to see my mom." Again he tried to tug free of Mrs. Rusillo's grasp.*

*"No!"*

*Skye frowned, confused. Mrs. Rusillo's voice didn't sound sweet and kind anymore; it was stern, harsh.*

*Skye looked at the fingers gripping his upper arm. Even as he watched, the pudgy, pale hands elongated. Every bone became visible and her fingernails turned into claws that grew and grew until they completely encircled his arm.*

*Horrified, Skye looked to the woman in white for help.*

*She smiled at him, a weird, calm smile that didn't reach her eyes. Her eyes looked dead.*

*"Come with me." Mrs. Rusillo pulled him toward the front door, and Skye struggled frantically with the thing she was becoming.*

*"No! Let me go!"*

*Pulling desperately to get away from her, he dropped the vase. In slow motion, the glass fell to the hardwood floor, breaking into tiny pieces. Water poured out like fresh tears. The flowers wilted immediately.*

*"See what you've done?"*

*The voice came to him as if from far away, deep and contorted, like it was being played at the wrong speed on a phonograph.*

*"Let go! Mom! Mom! Mama . . . !"*

*He felt himself screaming, felt his mouth moving, but he couldn't hear any sound.*

*Abruptly the scene changed and a hand shot out, striking him on the side of the head, and knocking him to the floor. Skye's father stood over him, huge and menacing, one burly arm raised and poised to strike again.*

*"Sniveling brat," his father growled, and the voice sounded exactly right, exactly like it always did. "That oughtta teach you not to bawl in the middle of the night. You ever wake me up again and I'll knock you through the wall."*

*"I want my mom."*

*"What did you say?" The whole apartment, the whole world, seemed to echo with the sound of his roar. He balled his hand into a fist and pulled it back—a warning and a threat.*

*"Ungrateful little bastard. No wonder your mother kicked off when she did. Having to deal with a little bastard like you. And what the hell am I supposed to do with you? Good for nothing... Just like a female, she didn't teach you crap."*

*"Shut up! You can't talk about my mother."*

*His father's face twisted with rage. The veins in his neck swelled like they were about to explode.*

*A huge cigarette-stained hand reached for the collar of Skye's shirt. "She didn't teach you anything, but I will."*

*Rage warred with fear in Skye's thin chest. "Shut up. Bastard! I hate you!"*

*The fingers closed around his collar and even as he was yanked off the ground with a force that nearly strangled him, Skye imagined all the ways he would fight back....*

He awoke by jerking up in bed, his hands clenched into tight fists, his biceps pumped for action.

It took Skye a moment to realize where he was, and a moment longer to calm the racing of his heart. Flight or fight. The adrenaline associated with the automatic survival response coursed through his body.

Sweat poured from his temples. Covered the sheets. Against his damp skin, the stale air in the motel room felt cold.

Pushing the limp blanket away, he sat on the edge of the bed and waited for his breathing to slow.

He hadn't had it in years—that particular nightmare. He hadn't thought about the flowers.

Bracing his palms on the edge of the mattress, he lowered his head. He didn't have to wonder what it all meant—the dream, the panic; he knew. He'd felt it all again since last night: that churning, miserable dread; the guilt and unbearable shame of not being able to help the one person you loved with all your heart. The only person who had ever needed you.

Skye no longer believed that a bouquet of flowers had the power to heal. He no longer believed that his failure to water his mother's primroses had in any way hastened her death.

But he knew that he'd caused her sorrow, and that sorrow, however fleeting, pressed against his own soul.

To love someone, to stay with them for any length of time meant that someday, somehow, you would hurt them. It was inevitable.

And that was what he could no longer tolerate. To be hurt himself was one thing, but to hurt someone else, someone he loved...

Lifting his head, he looked at the gray light reaching around the heavy curtains. Dawn.

He took a deep breath. Last night he'd phoned Rose and spoken just long enough to say he had a headache and wouldn't be able to see her. She'd asked if he had aspirin, wanted to bring him dinner. And he had snapped at her, because he didn't want anyone to be nice to him.

He closed his eyes, feeling older than he'd ever felt in his life and achingly, infinitely weary because he knew Janet was right.

There were times when the nicest thing you could do for someone was to leave them alone.

# Chapter Twelve

Someday, someday very soon, Rose vowed, she would start her day smelling like Chanel No. 5 rather than ham.

She finished carving the extra-thick slices she liked to serve for breakfast, heaped them on a platter, and covered the meat with plastic wrap. She hummed as she worked, giggling to herself when she realized what she was doing. It wasn't like her to hum at six-thirty in the morning, but today even smelling like cured pork couldn't dampen her spirits.

Nothing could. Not when there was so much to look forward to.

Poor Skye had sounded so tired last night. He said he had a headache and apologized for being irritable, but she wasn't upset. Disappointed that she wasn't going to see him, yes, but not upset. She was about to embark on the biggest adventure of her life: learning all about another person. His moods, his habits, what made him sad and what brought him joy. She was excited enough that even the sour moods couldn't upset her.

She grinned. Not yet, anyway.

After tucking the slab of ham back into the refrigerator, Rose opened a five-pound can of orange marmalade and started filling jam pots. With any luck, the day would speed by. And she had big plans for tonight.

Her dining room table was already set with candles and china and flatware. All the makings for Burgundy Stroganoff à la Rose waited in her refrigerator upstairs. All she needed was the man.

And she had him.

With a smile as broad as a double-wide mobile, Rose reveled in the knowledge. The man she wanted, wanted her.

She could have been nervous, sleeping beside Skye, but she hadn't been. Opening her heart and her life to a man had always seemed like a gargantuan risk, but then Skye had held her and she had never felt so safe.

She felt so good, in fact, she was going to make her special cinnamon-sugar muffins—and give the whole dang batch away to the first person who smiled real nice.

Giggling, she tapped a marmalade-laden spoon on the lip of the jam pot and went to collect the ingredients for her muffins.

A firm knock redirected her attention to the door.

"Skye!"

Checking the clock as she hurried over, Rose twisted the key in the lock and pulled open the glass door. Skye stepped across the threshold.

"You're early," she informed him happily. "But if you're interested in more hours, that can be arranged. I know the owner."

Skye's smile was brief. "I wanted to talk to you before you open."

Rose studied him for a moment, rapidly coming to two conclusions. First, that she would never tire of looking at him, even if the pleasure was hers for the next fifty years; and second, that something was wrong.

His deep blue eyes had shadows beneath them, and the under-eye area was puffy, as if he hadn't slept at all. Tired lines framed his mouth.

"Do you still have that headache you had last night?" she asked in concern. "I wish you had let me bring over a bottle of aspirin. I bet you never even took any. Here, I'll get you a couple right now."

He grabbed her arm before she could walk away. "Rose. I don't want any aspirin."

She shook a finger at him. "Stubborn," she admonished. "There's no point in being brave if it causes you to suffer."

"I don't have a headache."

"Oh. You look so tired, I thought..."

Skye let go of her arm and ran a hand through his shower-damp hair. "I didn't sleep very well."

For no particular reason, a frisson of foreboding zinged down her spine. "Well, you don't have to start so early today. We won't be *that* busy. You could even take the day off."

Skye looked at her, wishing he could take her in his arms.

He loved the way she looked each morning when he came in to work. A pretty blouse tucked into jeans, her short apron riding her hips, the long strings wrapped around her waist and tied in front in a knot, like she had better things to do than bother with a bow.

The picture she presented never failed to conjure up other images in his mind, visions of the tomorrows they could have together.

Ruthlessly he cut the image off. He steeled himself against the worry in her eyes. He was about to do the right thing....

Reaching into the pocket of his denim jacket, Skye withdrew a small, black velvet pouch. Loosening the silky drawstrings, he tipped the contents into his palm and held out his hand.

Rose looked down and smiled in wonder.

"It's beautiful."

A tiny enamel butterfly, barely the size of a dime, perched in the center of Skye's palm. Its pink and black wings rested half-raised, as if it had alighted on Skye's hand from a nearby garden and was pausing briefly before it flew away.

"It looks so real," Rose breathed, reaching a tentative finger to touch the lovely painted wings.

"I want you to have it," Skye said, raising it by a thin gold chain so that the butterfly hung suspended. "It belonged to my mother." Her brown eyes, large and full of awe, met his. "Oh, Skye. Are you sure?"

"I want you to have it," he stated again forcefully. "Turn around."

Rose presented her back and Skye placed the butterfly around her neck.

Facing him again, she ran her fingers reverently along the black body and over the pink-dotted wings. She felt overwhelmed as joy swelled inside her and her earlier reservations were forgotten. "It's so beautiful and delicate, but I've never seen a butterfly this spectacular. The black and the pink—"

"The color and the markings are accurate," Skye told her. "There's a farm in South Dakota. I don't know if it's there, anymore, but when I was a kid an old woman and her husband owned it. The woman had a greenhouse that she opened to the public. I was only eight the first time my mother took me to it. I didn't know why anyone would want to walk around a bunch of indoor plants."

His smile held sadness as well as humor.

"It wasn't just any garden, though. The old woman raised butterflies, hundreds of them, in every color, every combination you can imagine. I'd never seen anything like it. If you stood still, even for a moment, a butterfly would land on you, rest for a while and fly off again."

His humor evaporated, leaving only the sadness and a sobering, heart-stopping regret that stained his voice, making it rough and deep as he continued. "They never stayed long, not on me, anyway, but while one was there, it felt—" he willed her to understand the message in his words "—like I was standing in paradise."

"Why didn't they stay?" Rose whispered.

Skye shook his head. "I could never stand still long enough."

The fear that had snaked through her earlier took root now.

She stared at Skye with wide, distressed eyes. "Goodbye. You're saying goodbye."

Mutely, his own tongue leaden, he nodded.

"Why?" Rose stared imploringly, unable to fathom this sudden turn of events. "Why now? Two nights ago, everything was fine. What happened?"

She saw the muscles in his neck move when he swallowed. His voice was gritty. "I was kidding myself. We both were. And I was being unfair to you, pretending a relationship between us could work."

"Pretending?" Anguish sliced through her. To say that what they felt two nights ago wasn't real . . .

"It *can* work." Her exclamation pulsed with bald need. She didn't care. They had come too close to turn back now. "It *will* work."

"No." Skye forced a smile that was meant to be tender, but wound up being little more than a grim, humorless twist. "There's no future with me. There never has been." When she tried to protest, he cut her off. "We're too old for make-believe. I move around without having to answer to anybody, and that's how I like it. That's how it's going to stay."

Rose's head swam. "You said you felt something when we were together." She swallowed her pride. "I don't understand. You said everything was different now."

If possible, his expression became more grim. "I said a lot of things I shouldn't have. If I regret anything, it's that I led you on. I'm—"

"Don't! Don't you dare say you're sorry."

Rose searched Skye's face, looking for the information he wasn't giving her. Suddenly, she remembered what else he'd said Monday night. "You had something else to tell me, but you wanted to wait. What was it? Tell me now."

"It doesn't matter anymore."

"Of course it matters!" Her desperation acquired an edge of anger.

The clenching of his jaw was the only sign that her words affected him.

"You owe me an explanation, damn it!"

Skye didn't deny it, but he stood for a long time before he spoke, his eyes growing sadder and more weary with each passing moment. "Some people are meant to be in relationships. Some people are meant to settle down...and some aren't.''

"That's a lie." Rose shook her head. "That's what I've been telling myself for years—it'll happen if it's meant to be." A bubble of ironic laughter stuck in her throat. "Well, I've waited thirty years to find out what life has in store for me and let me tell you, it isn't much."

Tears stung her eyes. She blinked them away before she continued.

"You'll never know if something is meant to be until you make it happen and see if it works. That first night you showed up, I was wishing for something or someone I could care about. Completely. Well, I got it. And I don't care if it's 'meant to be.' *I* mean it to be."

This time when he spoke, the tenderness he felt reached his eyes. "There are situations, Rose, there are people not even love can fix."

The tears she'd been holding at bay filled her eyes. "That's not true."

"It *is* true."

More than anything else, it was the finality in his tone that made her feel cold and sick.

Rose reached for the clasp of the necklace. Working the catch, she freed the jewelry from around her neck and held his gift out to him, her fingers trembling.

"Take it," she said in a voice that shook with all the anger and frustration and sadness her body could hold. "I don't want to be a fond memory for you. I don't want to be anybody's *past*. Not until I've had a present."

When Skye refused to take the necklace, she moved forward and put it in the breast pocket of his jacket.

Stepping away, she bit back her misery and spoke as calmly and honestly as she could. "You're wrong. There are no people who aren't meant to have relationships.

Nobody is supposed to walk through life alone. I've been alone long enough to know.''

The lunch rush ended early. By 1:15, only a few stragglers remained at the counter.

It hadn't been much of a rush, anyway, Rose acknowledged as she closed the unused loaves of sandwich bread and bound them with twist ties. The slow lunch was probably a blessing. Her mind wasn't on cooking, and she didn't have Skye to help her anymore.

He'd left shortly after their confrontation. He wouldn't be coming back. She'd told him not to.

Rose lined the loaves neatly over the area where she made the sandwiches.

''You got any more coffee?''

Rose nodded, grabbed the pot and refilled Mill's cup. ''You're hanging around later than usual today,'' she remarked. ''What's the matter? You and Ray have a fight?''

''Naw, naw. I'm just feelin' lazy.''

Rose knew better. He'd been watching her with a worried frown lining his craggy face ever since she told him about Skye.

''I'm fine, Mill,'' she insisted. ''I've been handling the counter on my own for a year and a half. I guess I can do it again until the place sells.''

''Yeah.'' Mill grumbled into his coffee, uncomfortable with the topic of selling the emporium. ''Maybe what you need is a vacation. Go away for a couple of weeks, relax.''

Rose shrugged. ''Maybe. If I don't get any nibbles on the place.''

A trucker who'd stopped in for her macaroni casserole lunch special signaled that he was ready to pay his ticket, so Rose moved to the cash register.

She was straightening the singles in the cash drawer when a young man entered the store. Rose paid him little attention at first, except to note that he ought to have been in school this time of day.

When he stood uncertainly, glancing from her to the counter, she shut the drawer and addressed him. "Looking for something in particular?"

The boy hesitated. He was wearing jeans, a T-shirt and a brand-new letterman's jacket that was much too warm for the midday heat. Wiping a palm on his jeans in a purely nervous gesture, he nodded.

"Yeah." He cleared his throat. "Yes. I'm looking for a guy... he works here."

"A guy who works here?" Rose frowned. "Skye?"

The teen's gaze darted around the store. He jerked his head once in the affirmative. "Is he here?"

"What's your name?"

"Chad."

Chad's nervous fidgeting increased. He shoved his hands in the jacket's deep side pockets, a move so characteristic of the man he had come to see, Rose felt a sudden surge of sadness.

She wondered if Chad was a rodeo fan and Skye the idol he had ditched school to see.

"Well Chad," she began, sorry to disappoint him, "Skye is—"

Abruptly, she stopped. Chad pushed a lock of curly black hair out of his eyes... eyes as blue as midnight.

She studied the young man in front of her more closely.

"Is Skye expecting you?"

He shook his head.

The hair, the eyes, the shape of his jawline and brow...
Rose experienced a wave of recognition that felt eerily
like déjà vu.

Chad's glance flicked to the counter, lingering on two
younger men who were nursing sodas.

Rose's curiosity peaked. She jumped to a conclusion,
and it seemed outrageous, even to her. Yet, if she was
right...

Her heartbeat sped up. For once, she decided to let her
underworked intuition be her guide.

"Here, come over to the counter." She led Chad to a
seat next to Mill and made the introductions. "Chad's
looking for Skye."

Millard looked at the boy with interest.

"Will you fix Chad a sandwich or a shake—whatever
he wants," Rose asked her friend, adding with her expression, *keep him here.* Bemused, Mill nodded.

"Skye isn't here at the moment," she said to Chad,
"but I'm sure he'll be back." Her mind raced as she
wondered if Skye was still at the motel, and whether she
was about to do the right thing, or make a complete ass
of herself.

She offered a minute shrug to Millard's raised eyebrow. "I have to step out myself. Order whatever you
want in the meantime." She shoved her simple, one-sided
menu in front of the teen. "You're hungry, aren't you?"

Chad looked uncertain. "I guess, but—"

"Whatever you want. On the house. You can take care
of things for a while, Mill?"

"I've worked this place a time or two." He nodded.

Rose smiled gratefully. With her heart hammering
against her ribs, she rushed from the emporium.

The first thing she saw as she ran across the street was
Skye's truck.

Her heart pounded harder.

Outside the paint-chipped door to his room, Rose took a deep breath and said a quick prayer for guidance, then raised her hand and knocked. It couldn't have taken more than a few seconds for Skye to answer, but it felt like forever.

Surprise filled his face when he saw her. His eyes lifted past her to the emporium, as if the time of day alone made it hard for him to reconcile her appearance here.

"Mill's watching the store," she said, putting a hand on her hip when Skye merely stood there. "Well, are you going to invite me in?"

Indecision and regret warred with the surprise on his face. Rose was sure she could see him guarding himself against his softer feelings. He spoke with infuriating detachment. "We said everything there is to say. I'm getting ready to check out."

"Check-out was at eleven," Rose contradicted, allowing a healthy anger to fuel her words. "You're already paying for another day, so be a good host and let me in. And you can take that dark, hunted look off your face. I'm not here to try to change your mind about us."

The sheer unpredictability of her attack worked. After another moment's hesitation, Skye stepped back from the door, and Rose sailed past him, her characteristic reticence disappearing as she realized she had nothing to lose.

"That's better," she said, moving straight to the bed and seating herself. She folded her hands and waited for Skye to shut the door.

He did, then leaned against it.

"We haven't said everything there is to say," she contradicted, mentally crossing her fingers. If her suspicion about Chad was incorrect, she was going to feel pretty stupid in another minute, but so what? After a steadying breath, she took the plunge.

"You never told me about your son."

Her words had exactly the effect she'd hoped; the truth blazed across Skye's face. Rose felt teeming curiosity and an aching tenderness for the man in front of her. This was the first time she'd seen Skye look scared.

"He came into the emporium," she said quietly. "Looking for you."

Skye muttered an expletive. He crossed the few steps to the window and stared across the street. "When?"

"About ten minutes ago."

Skye's gaze flew to her. "Has he gone?"

"No," she said, assuring him. "He's still there. He won't be going anywhere for a while. Mill's plying him with sandwiches and milkshakes."

"What...what did he say?" Skye's voice was as hoarse as a four-pack-a-day smoker's.

"Not much," Rose admitted. "Only that he was looking for you. And he stared at a couple of men at the counter like there was a bounty on them."

"He's never seen me," Skye admitted heavily, pressing his thumb and forefinger against his brow. When he looked up again, his gaze was searching. "Did he ask for me by name?"

"Yes, of course." Rose was surprised by the sharpness of the question. "Skye, doesn't he know you're his father?"

"I'm not sure." Skye shook his head and turned to the window again. "I didn't think so. Did he come in alone?"

"Yes. Skye," Rose said, leaning forward over her knees, "I know you must have come to Wiedler because of Chad. But now you're leaving and he's never even seen you." On the brink of asking why, a new thought occurred to her. "Have you ever seen him?"

"I've gone to his school a couple of times. I waited outside."

Waited outside. "Don't you want to meet him?"

"Of course I do!" The answer came swift and vehement. "It's better for him this way." He raised a hand to rub the tension from his neck. "I don't know how he found out where I was. I told Janet where I worked over the phone, but she wouldn't have said anything."

"Is Janet his mother?"

"Yes."

Rose supposed that at this point the jealousy creeping through her was superfluous.

She wagged her head, longing to ask more questions, but realizing the timing was wrong. "I don't understand any of this," she said, "but I know your son is across the street. And you should be, too."

Slowly, his eyes riveted to the building on the other side of the street, Skye shook his head. His voice was so hushed, she had to strain to hear it. "Tell him I left."

"Tell him you left?" Rose sat up straight, palms braced on the edge of the mattress. "You've got to be kidding." She shook her head. "You amaze me. You'll face down two opponents in an unequal fight. You spent years riding two-ton animals that could have broken your neck. But when it comes to relationships, you've got your tail between your legs!"

Shock and fury flashed in his eyes, but Rose was too upset now to stop. All her hopes, all the dashed dreams— it all came down to this. Her future and the future of a young boy rested with a man who knew too well how to walk away.

"You waltz into town stirring up people's lives," she told him, not caring when tears came to her eyes, "but sticking around and caring for someone takes more courage than you've got. Well, we may be a little slow here in Wiedler, but I'd say that makes you the worst kind of tease." She pointed a shaking finger at the window. "I am not going across that street to lie to your son. If you want to walk away from people who only want you to love them, I guess I can't stop you. But I'm sure as hell not going to help!"

"*Want* to walk away?" Skye's gritted response shook his rigid body. "I don't *want* to." Frustration contorted his features. "I *have* to. Courage," he growled. "Lady, riding bulls is nothing compared to walking away when every part of you is begging to stay."

"Then don't go."

Longing and regret sharper than any pain he'd ever known knifed through Skye's chest.

*Courage.* It took all the courage in this whole godforsaken world to keep on loving when all he saw behind him was years of emptiness, and all that stretched before him was more of the same.

He would not walk across that street because he would cut off his arm before he hurt one more person he loved. He would not turn to Rose for the same reason.

Suddenly his mouth felt sandy and dry. His chest and throat ached with the emotion that was locked in his body.

What could he tell her? What should he say? His need to exonerate himself in her eyes meant nothing. She owed him no understanding. But he owed her.

She'd offered him trust, given him faith. He owed her any explanation that might minimize the pain he'd in-

flicted. He would give her the truth. It was all he had, and
it would explain his need to stay away. Once and for all.

He began slowly, keeping his sights on the emporium
as he sketched his past, working his way from both ends
to the middle. He told her briefly about his years in the
rodeo, where he'd spent his anger by punishing his body,
caring only infrequently whether he lived or died. Then
he backtracked and outlined the earlier days, when he'd
dropped out of school. He hadn't released his anger by
riding bulls back then; he'd released it by riding with the
wrong crowd.

And by having an affair with the least likely girl
around: the daughter of the town's mayor.

"When Janet got pregnant," he said, "I knew her father would just as soon kill me as see me married to his
daughter. But I wanted the baby, the whole family picture. I think I saw it all as a chance to begin again, get out
of the hell I'd been living in. I thought we could make it,
but Janet was smarter. She didn't think a trouble-seeking
eighteen-year-old was great father material." The bitter
twist of his lips was directed more at himself than the
mother of his child.

"She told me she was putting the baby up for adoption. Her parents were sending her to stay with an aunt
until the baby was born. She said she wanted it that way
and that she didn't think we should see each other again.
Looking back, that was probably the most mature decision she'd made since she decided to get involved with
me. But I had a little trouble accepting it at the time," he
said in a wry understatement.

"What did you do?"

"I went to the dance club she and her friends liked to
hang out in." Skye's hand clenched and flexed, but that
only hinted at the turmoil this memory evoked. "She'd

been dancing with some guy I'd never seen before, but I recognized him. He was just like me, a troublemaker. When I said I wanted to talk to her, he stepped in. I told him to mind his own business.... One thing led to another. I don't even know what happened to Janet. By the time he and I took it outside, she'd disappeared with her friends.

"I was angry." His voice was harsh with self-condemnation. "Angry with him, angry with her, angry at my whole loused-up life, because I knew I had no right to that baby, and I still wanted him. Funny, the last thing I remember thinking as we walked outside was that for once I didn't feel like fighting."

He made direct eye contact with Rose, wanting her to see exactly who he'd been. "Ordinarily I would have thrown the first punch. I never thought twice if someone wanted to fight.

"That night I didn't care. I fought because it was what I was used to. It didn't last long. He hit me. I hit him. We were in a parking lot, and he fell against a car. His head hit the side mirror. Hard." Skye's gaze shifted, grew distant. "You talk about courage. I remember telling him to get up, calling him a coward because I thought he was taking a dive. That's all courage meant to me then—fighting back. Not showing fear.

"He never did get up. And I went to prison for manslaughter." His expression hardened. "That's the past I bequeath to my son."

Rose felt his self-loathing. "What did Janet do while you were in prison?"

"If you're asking whether she came to see me, no. Like I said, she was smarter than I was. She knew when to cut and run."

"But she decided to keep the baby."

Skye nodded, turning back to the window. "All the more reason to stay away. How do you explain what I did to a little kid?"

"He's not a little kid anymore."

"He deserves more. He deserves better than to have to deal with his father's past."

"He deserves to feel loved by both his parents," Rose asserted adamantly.

"Janet loves him," Skye contended. "She's his parent."

"But he's aware of you now. Don't you see, Skye? You *choose* what legacy you leave your son. You can walk away and let him wonder about you the rest of his life. Or you can stay and show him that it's possible to forgive yourself. That's a wonderful thing to give a child. You can teach him that he has the power to change a bad situation into something good."

"Yeah." Skye's lips curved cynically. "The family of the guy who didn't get up might not feel the same way."

Rose shook her head sadly. "Please don't patronize me. I heard every word you said. I'm not whitewashing what happened. But you did not commit murder. You didn't want to kill anyone. You didn't even throw the first punch."

He scowled. "I didn't have to fight at all."

"True," Rose agreed. "So tell him that. Because someday he's going to be angry and hurt and believe that life is unfair, and he won't know what to do with his feelings."

"That's not quite my area of expertise, Rose," he reminded her tersely.

"You're an expert on what *not* to do," she reminded him right back. "If you stick around, maybe together you can figure out a better way."

He closed his eyes and shook his head, wanting to believe . . . not knowing how.

Skye thought of his own father, an evil-tempered man when he was sober, a violent one when he was drunk. From some of his father's ramblings, Skye knew that his grandfather had possessed the same uncontrollable temper and extreme difficulty relating to a child.

Skye, in turn, had reacted to his past and made mistakes as heinous as those of his sire. Like father, like son . . . and son? Or could one man break the cycle? He shook his head, hardly daring to hope.

"You really think a person can start over?" His words were so low, Rose had to strain to hear him.

Light and shadow played across his face, highlighting every line, every angle, every ounce of yearning. Rose knew his question was too important to answer lightly.

"Maybe not 'start over,'" she responded honestly after a moment. "But I think if we could make our pasts disappear, we'd lose more than we'd gain. We wouldn't know where we're weak, where we're strong, where we want to go from here. I think," she said softly, speaking to herself as well as to him, "that what we do is move on." She smiled gently and shrugged. "Everyone has a history. They don't have to be all good to be fruitful."

They fell silent then. Skye looked from the woman who sat on his bed to the building across the street, which housed his son, and wondered if moving on could redeem more than one life.

Rose looked at the man by the window and wondered the same thing.

# Chapter Thirteen

By five-thirty, the emporium was swept clean, the food was put away, and all that was left was the locking up.

Less than eager to return to her empty apartment, Rose lingered at the counter, treating herself to a supper of one giant chocolate chip cookie.

She picked absently at the semisweet chips, unable to keep her mind from wandering to Skye or from wondering what happened after he and Chad left the store that afternoon.

As long as she lived, she would never forget the look of pure tenderness and aching hope on Skye's face when Chad accepted the hand his father extended. Someday the manly handshake would turn into one of the hugs they'd missed all these years, she was sure.

Father and son were awkward and uncomfortable together, but that didn't worry Rose; she hoped it wouldn't worry them, either. They had left the emporium shortly after their initial hellos.

Rose plucked a chocolate morsel from the cookie and put it in her mouth, holding it on her tongue until it melted. The small bit of chocolate dissolved more quickly than she'd anticipated, and soon the sweetness was little more than a whisper.

*That, right there, is the problem with life,* Rose decided. Flavors, people, feelings—you could try and try to hang on to them, but still they shifted and changed, or disappeared altogether. All that remained was the memory.

Skye would come back, at least to say goodbye, Rose was certain, but he had a full plate now; he had a son to get to know.

And she had a restaurant to sell.

Her plans would remain the same. On that point, she stood firm. No more loitering in life. No more waiting for something to happen to her.

Moving on. Yes, she'd been talking as much to herself as to Skye.

The bells on her door jingled, and she swiveled on her seat, knowing whom she would see.

He was wearing his Stetson.

Standing just inside the door, Skye touched the brim of his hat in a gesture of respect. "Mind if I come in?"

Rose shook her head. Would her body ever respond normally when he walked into a room?

Skye approached the counter and took the stool next to hers. "Looks...interesting." He pointed to her cookie. "I guess all those dents are where the chocolate chips used to be?"

Rose glanced at her dinner and tried to collect herself. She wanted very much to be mature and philosophical about this. He was honorable. If he told her he needed space and time to deal with the new developments in his life, she wanted to respect that. Maturely, philosophically.

She smiled. "Some people eat their meat first, then their vegetables, then the potato. Some people twist their Oreo cookies, others dunk." Rose shrugged expansively. "I pull the chips out of my chocolate chip cookie."

Skye acknowledged her reasoning with a smile. He reached up and pushed his hat back. "I see you're closed for the evening," he said, looking around the counter, "but, ah...I saw your sign out front, and I didn't want to wait until morning."

"My sign," Rose repeated. She knew the one to which he referred, but if she had to talk about it tonight, she thought she might cry. "You mean the two-for-one corn dog sign?" she asked facetiously.

Skye shook his head. "No, ma'am. Although I'm sure the corn dogs are a bargain at any price. No, I was referring to the sign that says For Sale."

Rose said nothing. Mr. Pettifor had dropped off the For Sale notice late that afternoon.

"When I saw it," Skye confirmed, "I thought I'd better come right in. I wouldn't want anyone to beat me to it."

Rose looked at him quizzically.

"No one has beat me to it, have they?"

"No." Not certain what he was up to, she played along. "Are you really in the market for an old barn like this?"

Skye hitched a brow at her. "Do you really want to sell an old barn like this?"

Rose hoped she wouldn't turn teary. If she sold the emporium, all she would be able to take with her were the memories. Selling out meant moving on and saying goodbye.

"I really want to sell it," she said with forced conviction.

Skye studied her a moment, then nodded. "Then I'm really in the market to buy it. See, I've moved around a lot in my life. I believe I'm finally ready to settle down."

"You are?"

"I am." There was no hesitancy in his voice, not a jot of uncertainty in his steady gaze. "I thought I'd made a few mistakes in my life, but the one I almost made today takes the cake."

"What mistake?"

"Almost walking away from two people—Let's see, how did a very bright woman put it? Walking away from two people . . . who only want me to love them."

"Two people?" Rose whispered.

"That's what the lady said." His own voice lowered to a reverent hush. He searched her face. "I hope she still means it. If being alone was purgatory before, it'll be hell now, knowing what I'm missing."

Skye reached for her arms, lifting her with him as he stood. "After everything I told you, I wouldn't blame you if you ran in the other direction." His eyes burned with fiery longing. "But, Rose, I've spent most of my life wondering what would make me whole, and this afternoon I found it."

"Chad—"

"Is part of it," Skye affirmed, willing her to accept exactly what he was telling her. "But the healing, the thing that makes a relationship with my son seem possible, came earlier, in my motel room. In your eyes. I couldn't have crossed that street without you.

"If you want to sell this place, if you want to travel around the country or around the whole damn world," he said, his fingers absently beginning to stroke her upper arms, "I'll take you. If you'll let me. I love you, Rose."

She felt his fingers tremble against her arms with the admission. Rose's smile spread like sunshine.

"I love *you*." The words had been half a lifetime coming. Rose shook her head with a wonder of being able to say them unhesitatingly. "I love you!" Best of all, she had the rest of her life to mean them with all her might.

Their lips met and clung. It was a kiss neither wanted to end.

The glass door opened and closed, and still Rose and Skye continued to embrace. Later they would swear they never heard a thing.

"Well, don't that beat all!"

Millard's crackling voice finally broke the spell and jerked them apart. Beside Millard, Ray shuffled his feet and stared at the floor in embarrassment.

Mill smiled at their dazed, reddened faces. "Me 'n' Ray thought we'd come cheer you up, Rosalie, but it looks to me like you got all the cheer you can handle." He winked broadly, then nudged Ray with his elbow. "Don't you be lookin' now, Ray. Your eyes is too innocent for this kind of spectacle. I don't want you havin' no cardiac dilemma."

"Aww." Ray ducked his wrinkled, round head and grinned sheepishly.

"Glad to see you're back, son." Millard nodded at Skye before ushering himself and his old buddy to the door. He turned to Rose as he crossed the threshold.

"You want me to drop that For Sale sign off in front of the real estate office on my way home?"

Rose nodded. "Thanks. May as well now that I've found a buyer."

Mill's smile nearly slid off his face. "You what?"

"Yup." Rose arched a brow at her erstwhile employee. "Of course, he'll have to put his money where his mouth is. So far, he's all talk."

Mill grinned, his pleasure as plain as his relief. "See ya at breakfast." He closed the door firmly behind him.

Skye sat down again, expelling a long, shaky sigh. He pulled Rose between his legs, locking his fingers behind her back.

"I think *I'm* the one who's too old for this."

Rose laughed, a joyous sound that left her feeling like a breeze had swept through her body. "Not you," she said, removing his hat and smoothing a black curl. "You're just beginning."

He kissed her again, then drew back and glared at her archly. "So I'm all talk, huh?"

"That's all right. I like to hear you talk." Rose gave him a saucy grin. "By the way, how did Chad find out where you were? Not to mention who you are."

"He overheard his mother and grandfather." Skye shook his head. "Apparently they don't think much of my working as a 'soda jerk' and they discussed that, among other things, when they thought Chad was out of the house." He frowned. "Janet and I have a lot to discuss."

Feeling more confident than at any other time in her life, Rose decided not to broach the topic of Skye's ex-love for the time being. She seized instead on something she considered a serious slight.

"Soda jerk?"

Skye smiled. "I don't want to talk about that now. I only want to talk about us. And the right to be happy." He pulled her in until she was sitting on his lap with her arms about his neck. "I think someday soon I'll ask Chad if he wants to go shopping."

Skye trailed kisses along her collarbone.

"Hmm," she murmured, struggling to stick to the topic. "Shopping for what?"

"Tuxedos. I'd like to ask him to be my best man." His tongue teased the hollow of her throat. "Okay?"

Rosalie's heart beat like it had wings. "Are we talking about marriage here?" she asked hoarsely once she trusted herself to speak.

"Yeah." Skye pulled back and looked into her eyes. "I didn't see a sign out front, but would you by any chance be in the market for a husband?"

Rose tried gamely to look disgruntled. Oh, how she tried, but she couldn't suppress the grin nudging her cheeks. "You just want to get your hands on my emporium," she accused.

"Lady, I do want to get my hands on something, but it's not your emporium."

Skye growled in her ear, and Rose giggled delightedly.

"Before we look for the tuxedos," he said, "I think I'll pick up an engagement ring. Something gaudy, so all those truckers you feed will see that you're taken."

Rose fairly hummed with joy. Those truckers were no competition, but it warmed her down to her toes to have Skye think that they were.

"I think going shopping with Chad is a good idea," she said.

"Yeah?" Skye got to work kissing the other side of her neck.

"Mmm-hmm. Lots of male-bonding potential. I don't think you should look for an engagement ring, though."

"What?" Skye stopped kissing her and stared at the woman to whom he'd just proposed. "Why not?"

"Because I already know what I want for my engagement ring." She smiled at the relief that bloomed on his face.

"You do, huh?"

"Yes." Nodding dreamily, she laid her cheek against the pillow of his curly hair and imagined sleeping next to him every night for the rest of their lives.

Oh, yes, she knew.

A beautiful enameled butterfly was what she wanted— a reminder of the unexpected blessings that sometimes land in a person's life.

But this time the butterfly would be anchored to a band of gold, an endless circle that symbolized eternity.

*     *     *     *     *

# COMING NEXT MONTH

**#1150 WELCOME HOME, DADDY!—Kristin Morgan**
*Fabulous Fathers*
The Murdock marriage was over—or was it? Ross Murdock was
determined to win back his wife, Rachel, especially after discover-
ing another baby was on the way!

**#1151 AN UNEXPECTED DELIVERY—Laurie Paige**
*Bundles of Joy*
Talk about labor pains! Any-minute-mom-to-be Stacey Gardenas
was on an assignment when her baby decided to be born. And that
meant her handsome boss, Gareth Clelland, had to help deliver the
child.

**#1152 AN IMPROMPTU PROPOSAL—Carla Cassidy**
*The Baker Brood*
Colleen Jensen was desperate—and Gideon Graves was the only
one who could help her. But while searching for Colleen's missing
brother, would Gideon find the way to her heart?

**#1153 THE RANCHER AND THE LOST BRIDE—
Carol Grace**
Parker's sweet little girl made Christine feel like part of the fami-
ly—as did the sparks between her and the rugged rancher!
But could forgotten memories keep Christine from being a *true*
family member?

**#1154 AND MOMMY MAKES THREE—Lynn Bulock**
Long ago, Matt Viviano gave up on love and happy endings. But
the way Larissa Camden lit up his son's face was a dream come true,
and if Matt wasn't careful, he'd find himself in his own storybook
romance.

**#1155 FAMILY MINE—Elizabeth Krueger**
Marriage? Meredith Blackmoore refused to even *consider* marrying
Stoney Macreay. She could not ignore her daughter's wish for a
father and Stoney's desire for a family, but could she resist *her* own
need for Stoney?

## MILLION DOLLAR SWEEPSTAKES
## AND EXTRA BONUS PRIZE DRAWING

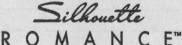

# As seen on TV!
# *Free Gift Offer*

With a Free Gift proof-of-purchase from any Silhouette® book, you can receive a beautiful cubic zirconia pendant.

This gorgeous marquise-shaped stone is a genuine cubic zirconia—accented by an 18" gold tone necklace.
(Approximate retail value $19.95)

# Send for yours today...
## compliments of ▼ *Silhouette*®
™

To receive your free gift, a cubic zirconia pendant, send us one original proof-of-purchase, photocopies not accepted, from the back of any Silhouette Romance™, Silhouette Desire®, Silhouette Special Edition®, Silhouette Intimate Moments® or Silhouette Shadows™ title available in February, March or April at your favorite retail outlet, together with the Free Gift Certificate, plus a check or money order for $1.75 U.S./$2.25 CAN. (do not send cash) to cover postage and handling, payable to Silhouette Free Gift Offer. We will send you the specified gift. Allow 6 to 8 weeks for delivery. Offer good until April 30, 1996 or while quantities last. Offer valid in the U.S. and Canada only.

## *Free Gift Certificate*

Name: _____

Address: _____

City: _____ State/Province: _____ Zip/Postal Code: _____

Mail this certificate, one proof-of-purchase and a check or money order for postage and handling to: SILHOUETTE FREE GIFT OFFER 1996. In the U.S.: 3010 Walden Avenue, P.O. Box 9057, Buffalo NY 14269-9057. In Canada: P.O. Box 622, Fort Erie,

---

## FREE GIFT OFFER                                    079-KBZ-R
ONE PROOF-OF-PURCHASE
To collect your fabulous FREE GIFT, a cubic zirconia pendant, you must include this original proof-of-purchase for each gift with the properly completed Free Gift Certificate.

---

**079-KBZ-R**

## SOMETIMES BIG SURPRISES
## COME IN SMALL PACKAGES!

# AN UNEXPECTED DELIVERY
### by Laurie Paige

Any-minute-mom-to-be Stacey Gardenas was snowbound at her boss's cabin—without a hospital or future husband in sight! That meant handsome, hard-nosed Gareth Clelland had to deliver the baby himself. With the newborn cradled in his arms, Garth was acting like a proud new daddy—and that had Stacey hoping for an unexpected proposal!

Coming in May from

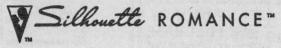

BOJ596

# You're About to Become a *Privileged Woman*

Reap the rewards of fabulous free gifts and benefits with proofs-of-purchase from Silhouette and Harlequin books

# Pages & Privileges™

It's our way of thanking you for buying our books at your favorite retail stores.

Pages & Privileges ™

**Harlequin and Silhouette— the most privileged readers in the world!**

For more information about Harlequin and Silhouette's PAGES & PRIVILEGES program call the Pages & Privileges Benefits Desk: 1-503-794-2499

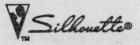

Silhouette®

SR-PP124